Gender Fraud

a fiction

Peg Tittle

Magenta

Gender Fraud: a fiction
© 2019 by Peg Tittle

pegtittle.com

First published 2020

978-1-926891-80-4 (print)
978-1-926891-81-1 (pdf)
978-1-926891-82-8 (ebook)

Published by Magenta

This is a work of fiction. Names, characters, places, brands, media, and incidents are either the product of the author's imagination or are used fictitiously. The author acknowledges the trademarked status and trademark owners of various products referenced in this work of fiction, which have been used without permission. The publication/use of these trademarks is not authorized, associated with, or sponsored by the trademark owners.

Cover design by Elizabeth Beeton and Peg Tittle

Formatting and interior book design by Elizabeth Beeton

Library and Archives Canada Cataloguing in Publication

Title: Gender fraud : a fiction / Peg Tittle.
Names: Tittle, Peg, 1957- author.
Identifiers: Canadiana (print) 20200202367 | Canadiana (ebook) 20200202375 | ISBN 9781926891804 (softcover) | ISBN 9781926891811 (PDF) | ISBN 9781926891828 (EPUB)
Classification: LCC PS8639.I76 G46 2020 | DDC C813/.6—dc23

Impact

"Edgy, insightful, terrific writing, propelled by rage against rape. Tittle writes in a fast-paced, dialogue-driven style that hurtles the reader from one confrontation to the next. Chock full of painful social observations ...." Hank Pellissier, Director of Humanist Global Charity

" ... The idea of pinning down the inflictors of this terror is quite appealing ...." Alison Lashinsky

It Wasn't Enough

"Unlike far too many novels, this one will make you think, make you uncomfortable, and then make you reread it ...." C. Osborne, moonspeaker.ca

"... a powerful and introspective dystopia .... It is a book I truly recommend for a book club as the discussions could be endless ...." Mesca Elin, Psychochromatic Redemption

"Tittle's book hits you hard ...." D. Sohi, Goodreads

Exile

"Thought-provoking stuff, as usual from Peg Tittle." James M. Fisher, Goodreads

What Happened to Tom

"This powerful book plays with the gender gap to throw into high relief the infuriating havoc unwanted pregnancy can wreak on a woman's life. Once you've read *What Happened to Tom*, you'll never forget it." Elizabeth Greene, *Understories* and *Moving*

"Peg Tittle's *What Happened to Tom* takes a four-decades-old thought experiment and develops it into a philosophical novella of extraordinary depth and imagination .... Part allegory, part suspense (perhaps horror) novel, part defense of bodily autonomy rights (especially women's), Tittle's book will give philosophers and the philosophically minded much to discuss." Ron Cooper, *Hume's Fork*

"I read this in one sitting, less than two hours, couldn't put it down. Fantastic allegorical examination of the gendered aspects of unwanted pregnancy. A must-read for everyone, IMO." Jessica, Goodreads

Sexist Shit that Pisses Me Off

"Woh. This book is freaking awesome and I demand a sequel." Anonymous, barnesandnoble.com

"I recommend this book to both women and men. It will open your eyes to a lot of sexist—and archaic—behaviors." Seregon, Goodreads

"Honestly, selling this in today's climate is a daunting challenge—older women have grown weary, younger women don't seem to care, or at least don't really identify as feminists, men—forget that. All in all a sad state of affairs—sorry." rejection letter from agent

Shit that Pisses Me Off

"I find Peg Tittle to be a passionate, stylistically-engaging writer with a sharp eye for the hypocritical aspects of our society." George, Amazon

"Peg raises provocative questions: should people need some kind of license to have children? Should the court system use professional jurors? Many of her essays address the imbalance of power between men and women; some tackle business, sports, war, and the weather. She even explains why you're not likely to see Peg Tittle at Canada's version of an Occupy Wall Street demonstration. It's all thought-provoking, and whether or not you'll end up agreeing with her conclusions, her essays make for fascinating reading." Erin O'Riordan

" ... a pissed off kindred spirit who writes radioactive prose with a hint of sardonic wit .... Peg sets her sights on a subject with laser sharp accuracy then hurls words like missiles in her collection of 25 cogent essays on the foibles and hypocrisies of life .... Whether you agree or disagree with Peg's position on the issues, *Shit that Pisses Me Off* will stick to your brain long after you've ingested every word—no thought evacuations here. Her writing is adept and titillating ... her razor sharp words will slice and dice the cerebral jugular. If you enjoy reading smart, witty essays that challenge the intellect, download a copy ...." Laura Salkin, thinkspin.com

"This was funny and almost painfully accurate, pointing out so many things that most of us try NOT to notice, or wish we didn't. Well written and amusing, I enjoyed this book immensely." Melody Hewson

"Not very long, but a really good read. The author is intelligent, and points out some great inconsistencies in common thinking and action …. may have been channeling some George Carlin in a few areas." Briana Blair, Goodreads

" … thought-provoking, and at times, hilarious. I particularly loved 'Bambi's cousin is going to tear you apart.' Definitely worth a read!" Nichole, Goodreads

"What she said!!! Pisses me off also! Funny, enjoyable and so right on!!!! Highly recommended." Vic, indigo.ca

Critical Thinking: An Appeal to Reason

"This book is worth its weight in gold." Daniel Millsap

"One of the books everyone should read. A lot of practical examples, clear and detailed sections, and tons of all kinds of logical fallacies analyzed under microscope that will give you a completely different way of looking to the everyday manipulations and will help you to avoid falling into the common traps. Highly recommended!" Alexander Antukh

"One of the best CT books I've read." G. Baruch, Goodreads

"This is an excellent critical thinking text written by a clever and creative critical thinker. Her anthology *What If* is excellent too: the short readings are perfect for engaging philosophical issues in and out of the classroom." Ernst Borgnorg

"Peg Tittle's *Critical Thinking* is a welcome addition to a crowded field. Her presentations of the material are engaging, often presented in a conversational discussion with the reader or student. The text's coverage of the material is wide-ranging. Newspaper items, snippets from *The Far Side*, personal anecdotes, emerging social and political debates, as well as LSAT sample questions are among the many tools Tittle employs to educate students on the elemental aspects of logic and critical thinking." Alexander E. Hooke, Professor of Philosophy, Stevenson University

What If? ... Collected Thought Experiments in Philosophy

"Of all the collections of philosophical thought experiments I've read, this is by far the best. It is accessible, uses text from primary sources, and is very well edited. The final entry in the book— which I won't spoil for you—was an instant favorite of mine." Dominick Cancilla

"This is a really neat little book. It would be great to use in discussion-based philosophy courses, since the readings would be nice and short and to the point. This would probably work much better than the standard anthology of readings that are, for most students, incomprehensible." Nathan Nobis, Morehouse College

Should Parents be Licensed? Debating the Issues

"This book has some provocative articles and asks some very uncomfortable questions ...." Jasmine Guha, Amazon

"This book was a great collection of essays from several viewpoints on the topic and gave me a lot of profound over-the-(TV-)dinner-(tray-)table conversations with my husband." Lauren Cocilova, Goodreads

"You need a licence to drive a car, own a gun, or fish for trout. You don't need a licence to raise a child. But maybe you should ... [This book] contains about two dozen essays by various experts, including psychologists, lawyers and sociologists ...." Ian Gillespie, *London Free Press*

"... But the reformers are right. Completely. Ethically. I agree with Joseph Fletcher, who notes, "It is depressing ... to realize that most people are accidents," and with George Schedler, who states, "Society has a duty to ensure that infants are born free of avoidable defects. ... Traditionalists regard pregnancy and parenting as a natural right that should never be curtailed. But what's the result of this laissez-faire attitude? Catastrophic suffering. Millions of children born disadvantaged, crippled in childhood, destroyed in adolescence. Procreation cannot be classified as a self-indulgent privilege—it needs to be viewed as a life-and-death responsibility ...." Abhimanyu Singh Rajput, Social Tikka

Ethical Issues in Business: Inquiries, Cases, and Readings

"A superb introduction to ethics in business." Steve Deery, *The Philosophers' Magazine*

"*Ethical Issues in Business* is clear and user-friendly yet still rigorous throughout. It offers excellent coverage of basic ethical theory, critical thinking, and many contemporary issues such as whistleblowing, corporate social responsibility, and climate change. Tittle's approach is not to tell students what to think but rather to get them to think—and to give them the tools to do so. This is the text I would pick for a business ethics course." Kent Peacock, University of Lethbridge

"This text breathes fresh air into the study of business ethics; Tittle's breezy, use-friendly style puts the lie to the impression that a business ethics text has to be boring." Paul Viminitz, University of Lethbridge

"Peg Tittle wants to make business students think about ethics. So she has published an extraordinarily useful book that teaches people to question and analyze key concepts …. Take profit, for example …. She also analyzes whistleblowing, advertising, product safety, employee rights, discrimination, management and union matters, business and the environment, the medical business, and ethical investing …." Ellen Roseman, *The Toronto Star*

more at pegtittle.com

Also by Peg Tittle

fiction

Impact
It Wasn't Enough
Exile
What Happened to Tom

screenplays

Exile
What Happened to Tom
Foreseeable
Aiding the Enemy
Bang Bang

stageplays

Impact
What Happened to Tom
Foreseeable
Aiding the Enemy
Bang Bang

audioplays

Impact

nonfiction

Just Think About It
Sexist Shit that Pisses Me Off
No End to the Shit that Pisses Me Off
Still More Shit that Pisses Me Off
More Shit that Pisses Me Off
Shit that Pisses Me Off

Critical Thinking: An Appeal to Reason
What If? Collected Thought Experiments in Philosophy
Should Parents be Licensed? (editor)
Ethical Issues in Business: Inquiries, Cases, and Readings
Philosophy: Questions and Theories (contributing author)

You can do this, she told herself as she sprinted—well, as she ran as fast as she could—along the road toward the curve in the distance. Heart thundering, lungs heaving, she made it to the curve, rounded it, and saw an intersection in the distance. You can do this, she kept telling herself, as she kept moving, getting closer and closer to the intersection … Yes, she was over sixty, just a tad over sixty, but she'd been running since she was thirteen, since she'd entered high school and discovered something called 'cross-country'. She'd done track in grades seven and eight, but— They ran through the forest! Or at least through the wooded parks on the edge of the city, which was, back then, the closest thing to forest she knew. She fell in love with it. The beauty. The quiet. The solitude. The rhythm. The distance. Between practices, she ran through her neighbourhood. Every day, further.

So she could do this. She'd been surprised to discover there wasn't a women's team at university, so she joined the men's team. But then discovered that women weren't allowed to run the long distances. It was the 70s. At all the cross-country meets, women did just three miles. Men did five. At the track meets, women couldn't run even the 5,000, let alone the 10,000; the longest event for them was the 3,000. But she kept running further, and further. On her own. She didn't know she was ready for a marathon in her late twenties. There was no internet.

She couldn't just google. She'd thought she'd have to be running twenty miles several times a week. Which is what she did. Which is why she was always tearing this or that.

Even so, she told herself, now trotting along a sidewalk, you can do this. It wasn't until her forties that she'd discovered that a total of fifty miles a week was sufficient preparation as long as she ran something over ten miles once a week. And by her forties, she'd been doing that for almost twenty years. So she ran her first marathon. At forty-five. Finished in under four hours.

As she approached the intersection, she could feel her heart still pounding, her lungs still straining. Okay, so you don't have the cardiovascular anymore, and you definitely don't have the flexibility, you'll be the tin man for days, but you've still got the strength. And the stamina. Because even at sixty, she'd been walking ten to fifteen miles every day, through the forest behind her cabin. You just have to get to forest, she told herself, you just have to lose whatever vehicles will be following you, and then you can walk. She stopped briefly to read the street signs, got her bearings, and was relieved to find herself at the south end of the city. She headed left. She could cut through the Walmart parking lot, then it was just a short bit to Seymour, which was the first exit, if you were coming from the south. She was jogging now. Limping, actually. It had been years since she'd run on sidewalk, on pavement. She was going to have shin splints. For the rest of her life if she didn't get into forest soon. Scrub bush, at least.

But she would be. Soon. There was forest on both sides of the highway all the way from her cabin to North Bay. Ergo, she grinned, all the way from North Bay to her cabin. It was 80km by highway. Probably more if she stuck to the forested edges. She could do 20km a day. She'd be home in four days. She could find safe places to sleep along the way ... Thank god it wasn't winter. The bear would be hibernating, but there would be wolves, and coyotes had moved up from the south … Though, now that she thought about it, they were unlikely to live, or hunt, this close to the highway.

A year ago, she would've just hitch-hiked. A year ago, she was stupid. Out of step. Behind the times. Now, she understood that there was a good chance that anyone who stopped to pick her up would report her. Unless it was a woman who stopped. But, she grimaced, it could be illegal for women to drive now. It suddenly occurred to her that an unescorted woman might attract attention. Especially a sixty-year-old woman who was running. Even if she *had* been dressed for it. She abruptly slowed to a walk, her knees screaming.

And then it occurred to her that she couldn't go home. That would be the first place they looked. Well, she could set up some sort of alarm system, prepare an escape route … into the crawl space, maybe. No, wait! Sam had turned his little cottage into a year-round rental, then decided it was too much trouble, to manage the renting of it. She still had the key he'd given her when she'd confessed that she often stopped at his place on her way back, having paddled the ten mile stretch of river past the end of the lake, to sit and watch the sunset. "Have a beer while you're here," he'd said. "Make yourself at home." Okay, she would, yes. She ventured a small smile.

You can do this, she told herself again.

It had happened so quickly. One day, she was walking along the dirt lane, as she did every day, along the fifty metres from her cabin to the path that led deep into the forest, dressed as she always was, sweatshirt over a tshirt, baggy cotton cargo pants, thick socks, and track shoes. She had a small pack belted around her waist, that held her ID, a small pad of paper and a pen, an alarm and, in case that didn't work, bear spray, and a flashlight if she did something stupid and took longer to get out. Bug spray in season. Earplugs for Thursdays when the gun club had their get-togethers, a shot every six seconds, echoing for miles and miles. Once when they'd started early, it had been sheer hell for the hour it took to get back inside her cabin, windows closed, music on.

She hadn't had to use the bear spray. A bear did catch her by surprise one day, as she no doubt did it, but it just growled and took off running. She'd also come across a momma bear and its two cubs, but they were far enough away that she noticed in time to stop. They were on the path ahead of her, the only way out, so she just stood there, patiently, to let them go where and when they wanted. Tassi had been so good, content to be held in her arms—they must've been upwind and too far away for her canine nose and eyes to notice them. After a while, she carried on, talking in a singsong voice to let Momma know where she was and, hopefully, to convey her harmlessness. That had always worked with the dogs who'd come charging at her on her long-distance runs. Back when.

She'd also met a wolf one day. A juvenile by the way it was moving, so easily. It had been trotting along the path toward her, oh what a wonderful day—she'd been thinking pretty much the same thing—and when they rounded the curve to find themselves suddenly face to face, they both came to a sudden and complete halt. Astonished. As for her, also delighted. The creature was absolutely gorgeous, its coat a mix of cream, tan, and chestnut. It considered her, then simply turned around and trotted back the way it had come.

The only other animal she'd come across—aside from the numerous, though decreasing numbers of, squirrels, rabbits, and grouse—was a young moose. Like the bear, it too had just taken off when it heard her.

The day it happened, she was a few feet from the path when a car coming down the hill pulled up next to her. Was a time she'd've waited, ready to be helpful, to offer directions, to tell the driver 'No, you can't get to the highway from here, it's a dead end, you have to go back—'

"Are you Kat Jones?" The uniformed man in the passenger seat had quickly gotten out to stand before her, blocking her way onto the path. He was young—that is to say, under forty—and clean-cut.

"Yes." So?

"Would you come with us, please?"

What? "Why?"

The uniformed man in the driver's seat was also out. And standing behind her.

"We've received reports."

This wasn't making any sense. "Reports of what?"

He flashed a badge. "You are hereby under arrest for Fraudulent Identity."

"Under arrest? For *what?*"

"Fraudulent Identity. Section 380(1) of the Criminal Code. Subsection 4(a). Gender Fraud."

The second one reached for her arm before she had time to process— Certainly before she had time to get out her bear spray.

"You're presenting as male," the first one explained, "when, in fact, you're female. That's fraud. And a criminal offence."

The second one pulled her arms behind her, bound her hands together with one of those black plastic zip ties she'd often used around her cabin, then forced her into the back seat. Just like that. Her world ended.

It hadn't even occurred to her to make a run for it.

She never did find out who had reported her. It could have been Chuck, who lived down the lane. Nancy's husband. When she'd left a print-out in their mailbox, informing them of the toxicity of the smoke that blew her way every time they burned their leaves—something they often did, forcing her inside—and there was no reason they couldn't simply rake them into a corner of their one-acre lot and leave them to decompose—which was actually better, ecologically, than burning them—he'd been enraged. He'd knocked on her door and when she'd opened it— foolish, yes—he'd stepped inside without invitation and proceeded to yell at her, thrusting out his massive ex-footballer chest and punctuating his words with a jabbing finger. When she'd tried to respond, to engage in a civil conversation, he'd screamed at her to "Just Shut Up and Listen!" and a few moments later concluded his tantrum by calling her a cunt.

Or it could have been Mike, the guy who owned the property across the cove. When he started cutting down the trees along the shoreline, she'd called the Ministry to ask whether there were any by-laws against that. So the next time he saw her, he too screamed at her. Gave her a shove and called her a bitch. And kicked Tassi.

Or it could have been Alfred. He'd wanted to hire her to clean his house; she'd declined. She already had a job, with a company in Princeton, writing logical reasoning and critical reading questions for the GRE. He hadn't known that. And why would he? It's not like she walked around proclaiming it to the 'hood, and no one had ever invited her to dinner or whatever. She didn't ... fit. He'd just assumed: she was a middle-aged woman, ergo.

Or it could have been Don, who owned the cottage two lots down from her and the empty lot next to her. She'd told him, thirty years ago, when she'd bought her cabin—a cabin on a lake in a forest!—that if he ever wanted to sell the empty lot, she'd buy it. The previous summer, she'd had occasion to speak to him because he kept letting his dog crash his way through her fence—admittedly a sorry affair of chicken wire strung from tree to tree—but it did the job, which was to keep Tassi safe inside—with the added bonus of being virtually invisible. His dog was big and young and unruly, whereas Tassi was relatively small and, by then, elderly. And although the dog's intent was to play, Tassi would've been hurt if Kat hadn't intervened. Three days after she'd asked Don—yes, with some vehemence—to keep his dog on his own property, a 'For Sale' appeared on the empty lot, and when she'd called to make an offer, he said he had no intention of *ever* selling it to *her*. She'd been anxious for weeks, knowing that she'd have to move, give up her little paradise, if someone bought the lot for a permanent residence.

They'd be too close: her solitude would be forever ruined. Even if they'd bought it just for seasonal use … If they had screaming kids or ATVs or snowmobiles or late night parties or used a generator instead of paying for an electrical hook-up … The sign eventually disappeared, and a year later someone told her he'd had no intention of selling it; he'd just wanted to upset her.

Or it could have been the guy who'd called out at her from his fume-belching ATV, when she was picking up the litter along the trail—as she often did, partly just to do her bit to keep the trails clean, but, eventually, mainly because *she* liked it better *without* the beer cans and the fast food containers and the cigarette butts—that it was 'Good to see she was good for somethin'!' She hadn't understood the comment until it was explained it to her: the man had probably thought she was a lesbian and so, since she wasn't any good for sex …

Yes, she lived in what she privately called 'a hostile neighbourhood.' But to be honest, she wasn't convinced it was just her neighbourhood. Men everywhere seemed to take offense when a woman spoke up, challenged them in some way. Or when she didn't at least *pretend* to be sexually available to them. Women weren't much better, either treating her like a kid, presumably because she wasn't married with kids of her own, or treating her like she was, in some way, off-putting. She didn't understand it. And yes, she was hurt by it.

So yes, she'd become a hermit. At sixty, she'd had enough, quite enough, of her uneducated, thick-skulled, and downright dangerous neighbours. And as for the world beyond, she found kin online. Sites like *I Blame the Patriarchy* and *Feminist Current* became her community. They were frequented by intelligent women who offered insightful discussion. Women much like her, she imagined. Radfem, for the most part. Probably over forty, for the most part.

And she was content. To live so alone. Though, actually, she didn't live alone. Well, hadn't lived alone until just recently. Tassi, her sole and constant companion, the love of her life, had died after fourteen years of happy, fourteen years of … sheer joy. A tumour had developed in her urethra. Malignant, aggressive, inoperable. Two months later, at the end of an absolutely wonderful day together, Kat had had her euthanized, to spare her the last stages of transitional cell carcinoma. And she was still … convalescing.

Maybe that's why she hadn't really noticed the car until it had pulled up beside her.

"Where are you taking me?" she asked, after the initial shock had worn off. They were on the highway, heading north. The nearest police detachment was south, in Burks Falls. But at least they weren't headed to Barrie or Toronto, two and three hours away. Already her shoulder was hurting. She should have asked them to bind her hands in front rather than behind. Thirty years of kayaking and snow shovelling had done something rather permanent to her rotator cuff.

"North Bay. You'll appear before a Justice of the Peace by end of business today."

"And then? How do I get back home?"

The responded with silence. And maybe a hint of laughter.

An hour later, the officer behind the wheel pulled into an underground lot that led into to a secured entrance area. The other one helped her out of the back seat and, holding firmly onto her arm, then led her through one, then another, set of doors into what was obviously some sort of processing area. He handed some paperwork to the officer behind the counter, then left.

The processing officer took her photograph, fingerprints, and a DNA sample, then led her to an adjoining room that had benches along three walls.

"Have a seat," he said. "It may be a while."

"Wait—"

He turned.

"Can you undo these ties? Or at least bring them to the front?"

"Sorry, no can do."

"But—"

He locked the door behind him.

A few hours later, it looked like she'd be spending the night. Surely if her case hadn't been called by what she guessed was around five o'clock, it wouldn't be called until the next day.

"Excuse me," she called out to the officer who had relieved the day shift.

He looked up from the other side of the reception counter. It was the limit of his acknowledgement. Of her existence.

"Could you please undo these ties. I've lost almost all circulation, and by morning, you may have to amputate both arms. I'm serious."

He merely grunted. But he did snip the ties. She almost screamed as the blood rushed back into her arms, setting her nerves on fire.

She'd missed supper. But she wasn't hungry.

What she was, was tired. Dead tired. Her body wasn't used to this kind of stress. So when she stretched out on the bench, she actually fell asleep.

Next morning, she could barely move for the pain and stiffness in her neck, her shoulders, her hips.

But move she did, led from the holding cell, along several hallways, into an elevator (yes, thank you!) (though a few flights of stairs might have loosened her up a bit), up to the third floor. Down a hall to a row of chairs outside Courtroom #5.

"Wait here," she was told. "Your lawyer will come get you."

Her lawyer?

The Courthouse in North Bay was not terribly imposing. She'd driven by it several times. But it was, nevertheless, official, and after a while, an armed guard came out of the room.

"Ms. Jones?"

"Yes."

"Come with me, please."

She was led into the dead-quiet room, up the centre aisle, to one of the two tables facing the Judge. A young woman at the table, smartly dressed in an ivory skirt and tailored jacket over a pale pink blouse, glanced at her and nodded.

"All rise. Justice Richard Meyers presiding. Court is now in session."

The young woman stood, then pulled Kat to her feet beside her.

"The Court calls Katherine Elizabeth Jones."

Confused, Kat stayed on her feet. Beside, presumably, her lawyer.

"Cynthia Seder, Your Honour, representing Katherine Elizabeth Jones."

The Justice nodded, and the Clerk continued.

"Katherine Elizabeth Jones, you are charged with Gender Fraud, pursuant to The Criminal Code of Canada, Section 380(1), revised, Subsection 4(a). How do you plead?"

What? Already? She glanced over at the young woman. Who nodded again, ambiguously. But they hadn't had a chance to speak. Well, she supposed her plea didn't need any discussion.

"Not guilty."

The Justice looked up at her in surprise.

"Do you dispute the facts in evidence? To wit," he read the record of arrest, "that you were, *are*," he looked at her, pointedly, "wearing men's clothing, that you are not wearing make-up, that your hair is short and undone, that you are not wearing any jewelry, that you are unmarried, that you do not have any children, that you have had your breasts removed, that you have had your reproductive capacity nullified via tubal cauterization, and that you have pursued an advanced academic degree?"

She was stunned. How had he gotten all that information about her? And why? And when? It must have taken a while … Which meant …

"In Philosophy, no less."

And if she were a man, that advanced academic degree, in Philosophy no less, would be evidence in *favour* of—well, anything.

"No," she said, trying desperately to get up to speed, "I dispute the interpretation of the facts. Your Honour. I was, *am*, not intending to defraud anyone. I am not intending to deceive anyone about my identity." She stared at her lawyer. Her absolutely useless lawyer.

"You are female, is that correct?"

"Yes."

"Then absent intent to deceive, your appearance and demeanour would be feminine."

What?

"And it is not. The court orders six months treatment in a psychiatric facility."

"Wait, *what?*"

The Judge banged his gavel, and the bailiff called the next case.

"I don't understand," Kat turned to the young woman, as two officers of the court approached her. "I'm being *committed?* Not just fined or …"

"Conditions justifying involuntary commitment to a psychiatric facility include gender dysphoria," she explained, "and gender fraud is considered conclusive evidence of gender dysphoria."

What?

"Can't we appeal? Prove my mental capacity?" Because she could surely do that. GRE and all that.

"That would apply in the case of danger to oneself or inability to care for oneself. But in the case of Gender Fraud, you're considered a danger to others."

What?

"How so?"

The young woman didn't answer.

"Wait—" Kat said as one of the officers gripped her arm and began to lead her away.

"Trust me," the young woman assured her, "you'd rather be incarcerated in a psychiatric facility than in a prison."

"Are you sure?" Kat said, looking over her shoulder.

"We'll appeal, of course, but … that'll take time. Good luck!"

What??

Kat was escorted—pulled and shoved actually, as her hands were zip-tied again, but at least in front this time—out of the room through a different doorway, into another elevator that descended one, two, three, four floors, then opened into an underground parking lot. This couldn't be happening, she thought. When she was able to think at all.

She was forced into the back of a transport van. Two women sat on a bench along the left side of the van, their hands, similarly shackled, in their lap. Kat was directed to the bench along the right. The door was closed. And locked.

"Either one of you know what the fuck is going on?" Kat asked. Absurdly. Why would they know about her case?

One of the women was sobbing, the other looked drugged. Neither one responded.

Half an hour later, another woman was brought into the van. Then another. And another. Only one was able to speak, and she seemed as stunned as Kat.

Six was apparently maximum capacity. "That's it!" she heard someone call out. The back panel of the van was slapped a couple times—why did guys do that?—and a minute later, it was moving. Presumably toward the psychiatric facility. What the fuck.

What happened next, when she arrived at the psychiatric facility as a court-ordered admission, was pretty much what she'd expected. She was taken into a small room. She was asked to empty her pockets, but everything she'd had with her was in her waist pack, which had already been taken. Next, she was subjected to a body cavity search, followed by a chemical shower. Probably for lice and what have you. She was given a paper gown to wear. Then a DNA swab was taken. And a blood sample. Presumably to test for contagious diseases such as HIV. She was photographed. And fingerprinted.

"If you'll just wait here for a few moments," the woman said, smiling—god knows why, "your counsellor is on her way."

"My what?"

"Every resident is assigned a counsellor. In addition to the psychiatrist you'll see once a week."

After a few moments, a woman appeared in the doorway. She looked like she was in her thirties, but she also looked like she'd been born in the 20s. Because she looked exactly like her mother had looked, in the 50s. The hairdo, the lipstick and rouge, the plucked-quizzical eyebrows, the tasteful earrings (as her mother would have called them), the string of pearls, the belted dress with a full skirt ... She even wore an apron. It was all so very ... odd.

"Hello, Katherine?" She smiled. Of course she did.

"Kat."

"But Katherine is such a pretty name."

"It may be, but I prefer Kat."

The woman made a note on the pad of paper she took from the pocket of her apron, then introduced herself. "I'm Mary-Anne, and I'll be your counsellor."

"What does that mean, exactly?"

"It means I'm the one who will help you adjust," she smiled. "On a daily basis. You'll also be seeing Dr. Gagnon, weekly."

"Adjust to what?"

"To life here and," she waved her hand, "out there. Eventually. We hope."

"But I was adjusted. To life … out there." She resisted the temptation to wave her hand.

"Well, no," Mary-Anne said gently, "you were living like a man. And you're a woman. That's what I'm here to help you with. Living like a woman."

Oh god, what rabbit hole had she fallen into?

"If you'll come with me," she said cheerfully, no doubt because permanent cheer was surely part of living like a woman, "we'll get your physical out of the way first. I don't imagine you'll want to walk through the facility in a paper gown, so I've brought you some clothes. Tomorrow you can take some time to pick out your wardrobe."

"Why can't I just wear my own clothes? I mean, this isn't a prison, right?" No need for the bright orange jumpsuit. Though, truthfully, she would've been relatively happy with that.

Mary-Anne just smiled, and handed her a medium-sized gift bag. Kat looked inside. And saw a dress. Oh god. She hadn't worn a dress since grade ten. With knee socks, she'd always felt so exposed, but wearing leotards was worse, they were so clingy and forever twisting on her legs. When she was in grade eleven, the school allowed girls to wear jeans. Most wore Levis, which were close-fitting on the thigh and a little flared at the bottom, but fortunately 'painter pants' made by Lee were also in style, offering a loose, baggy fit in a lighter denim. Kat loved her painter pants.

She gingerly pulled out the dress—a lavender flower print, no less—and then saw the bra that had been tucked underneath. She burst out laughing. For one, not since university. She was small, and her twice weekly work-outs in the weight room, along with her gymnastics coaching, had kept her pecs in good shape. Even as she aged, snow shovelling and kayaking ... And for two—

"Did I get the size wrong?" Mary-Anne asked.

"I don't know," Kat finally said, still holding the dress. "I don't actually know what size I am." Because—who cared? Mary-Anne made another note. In grade ten, Kat had worn a size twelve. Which was why, when she'd started hearing her students—in her forties, she'd become an sessional at Nipissing University and could finally say good-bye to the precarious patchwork of part-time jobs— When she'd started hearing her students say they were a size four or a size two, she thought surely that can't be right. Even with anorexia. When they started saying they were trying to become a size zero, she laughed. What was next, a *negative* size? Yes! Agree to become invisible! Agree to *actual* female erasure! Young women were such idiots. Kat was often admonished, on feminist blogs open to comments, for her lack of solidarity, but she was having none of that. Once you hit your late teens, you should be thinking for yourself, and while she didn't expect anyone to 'wake up' overnight, she had no patience for fools of either sex.

She looked at the label on the dress. Her painter pants had been a 28/30, then a 30/30, and her cargo pants, a 32/30. A few months ago, she'd started wearing 30/30 again; she'd lost fifteen pounds from the moment of Tassi's diagnosis to her death and another ten since. Her t-shirts and sweatshirts were generally a large. No help there.

"Well, why don't you try everything on and see?"

"Do you have any other outfits? Just a simple pair of pants and a … top?"

"No, I'm afraid not. Everything we do here is intended to help you."

"Help me … how?"

Mary-Anne didn't respond. Except to make another note.

If you wanted to help me, Kat thought, you'd let me wear comfortable clothes.

"Well, I don't need the bra." She stood up then, faced Mary-Anne, and shrugged the paper gown off her shoulders.

Mary-Anne gasped. "Oh. I didn't— Have you already had bottom surgery as well?"

"What?" Kat was momentarily confused. "I didn't get top surgery! I mean, I did, I guess, but— I'm not transsexual. It was a bilateral mastectomy. For breast cancer. Stage zero."

"Oh, I'm so sorry. We can get you a mastectomy bra."

"Isn't that a bit of an oxymoron?" she asked.

Mary-Anne didn't understand.

"Since I've had a mastectomy, I don't *need* a bra," Kat explained.

"But—" Mary-Anne stuttered, "of course you need a bra! Back in a minute—" She hurried out of the room.

Kat just sat there. Her mind racing. And stuck. At the same time.

Mary-Anne rushed back into the room. "Here you go!"

It was a bra with built-in falsies.

"Seriously? You expect me to wear this? Why?"

Mary-Anne couldn't say.

Kat could. "You want to sexualize me. And why do you want to do that?"

Mary-Anne couldn't say.

Kat could. "Because sexualizing women is a way to subordinate them. And *why* do you want to do that?"

Mary-Anne couldn't say.

Kat could. "Because men's power, men's privilege, depends on it. Well, fuck that."

Mary-Anne gasped. And made a note.

Kat tossed the bra onto the chair. "I'm not wearing it."

"But— You … you *have* to."

Was it so incomprehensible? A woman not performing femininity? Apparently.

"No. I don't *have* to. The fact that I haven't been doing so for decades is proof of that."

"I mean—   Please. It's for your own good. I'm just trying to help."

Kat was tired. Suddenly very tired. If it meant she could get on with the intake, get to her room, get into a bed … She put on the clothes. What choice did she have? She felt ridiculous. She felt like she was going to a Hallowe'en party. Though actually, she recalled, for the only Hallowe'en party she'd ever gone to, back in university, she'd simply put on a flannel shirt with her jeans, added a cowboy hat, and called it a day. Her friend was not impressed. But even as a kid, playing dress-up had *so* not appealed to her. She just couldn't— She felt so strange being, appearing to be, someone other than herself.

She was *so* not going to make it out of here.

Mary-Anne handed her another bag. "Some shoes," she said.

Kat opened the bag. Of course. A pair of high heels. Again, she sighed, not since grade ten, and even then, *low* heels. Penny loafers, for the most part. Saddle shoes for a while when they made a comeback.

"I can't walk in these."

"Sure you can!"

"No. I can't. I've never worn heels."

Another note.

"And at sixty, I'm not about to start. I'll twist an ankle or something."

"Well ..." Mary-Anne was thinking, "I suppose a pair of ballet slippers would do."

"No, they don't have any cushioning. My feet have taken a lot of pounding over the years, and now unless I have some sort of shock absorption ..." About ten years ago, when she'd had to slam on the brakes, a piercing pain shot up through her leg. Her physician ruled out muscle, ligament, and tendon issues—and Kat concurred, as she'd experienced all three and this had been something quite different—and suggested that maybe the sheath of one of her nerves had simply worn thin. It would explain the occasional, out-of-the-blue pain that started happening not only when she had to slam on the brakes, but whenever she stepped on her right foot the 'wrong' way. That's why she had wall-to-wall carpeting in her cabin and why she always wore thick socks. She'd tried slippers, but didn't like the ... confinement. As for outdoors, track shoes. Good track shoes. Always.

She stared at the thin soles of the high heels. No shock absorption whatsoever. And the facility probably had hard tile flooring everywhere ... She suddenly had an idea. "How about a pair of nurse's shoes?"

"Well, there might be some available," Mary-Anne said, "but at least for now, I'm afraid you'll just have to *try* ..." As if Kat simply wasn't making the effort. As if women who didn't wear make-up, who didn't at least *try* to look good, were lazy. Kat sighed. It was an attitude she recognized.

It took half an hour to get to the infirmary. Which was just down the hall and around the corner. Kat didn't want to take any chances. And yes, she exaggerated her difficulty a little. She hugged the wall, trailing one hand along it for balance, and for each step, lifted her foot straight up so as not to catch the heel and then put it down full weight so as not to teeter.

"Try putting one foot directly in front of the other," Mary-Anne had encouraged. "You want to walk in a straight line."

"No, I do not. Want to walk in a straight line." What was next, practising with a book balanced on her head?

Mary-Anne surely made another note.

The institution was clean, Kat was happy to see. But very white. Winters were long in the north, and a few years prior, she'd become so tired of nothing but white and dark green and grey and white and dark green and white and grey that she'd bought some diffraction sheets to hang in her cabin windows so when she looked out, she saw rainbow streaks. She discovered, with delight, that she could buy a pair of clip-ons for her glasses that did the same thing, and she often wore them while walking through the winter wonderland forest. Because her cabin was tucked in a cove, she couldn't see the sunset—a great disappointment, though the privacy of her location was good compensation and, at least for six months of the year, she could make sure she was out on the lake at sunset. So, and, she filled her cabin with orange and magenta and fuchsia—the carpeting, her bedding, the covers on her couch and her tv lounge chair— the only pieces of furniture other than her desk and its chair ... God, she missed her cabin already. How was she going to get through this? Not being able to see the sparkling water all day— Not being able to go kayaking or walking every afternoon, all afternoon— It was going to send her into some sort of withdrawal.

They passed several offices and various rooms of all sizes— recreational areas?

"All of the residential rooms are on the upper floors," Mary-Anne said, in a perky tour guide voice. "On the ground floor, we have our administrative offices, the infirmary, the cafeteria, a few on-site services, and the classrooms."

Classrooms?

The infirmary, she saw once they got there, was impressive. Clean. Spacious. Staffed. Supplied. Perhaps they'd spent so much effort on that in order to minimize the need for patients, residents, to go off-site. She wondered what the mentioned 'on-site services' included.

Kat was given a clipboard on which there was a five-page questionnaire to fill out. She checked most of the 'no' boxes and listed her few surgeries: as a child, she'd had her tonsils removed; in her twenties, she'd broken her elbow when a car hit her motorcycle, requiring the insertion, and later the removal, of a pin; at thirty, she'd gotten herself sterilized—neutered, as she liked to think of it; and in her early fifties, she had the bilateral mastectomy. She'd had no illnesses to speak of, she wasn't taking any medications …

"No medications at all?" the nurse asked when she scanned her questionnaire. "You're … sixty-one."

"Yes. No. Just a multi-vitamin, one of those eye tablets when I think of it—"

"You mean the AREDS formulation? For macular degeneration?"

"That's it."

"You've been diagnosed?"

"No, it's just a precaution." Because if she ever became unable to read, to see … "I understand it's recommended for people over fifty."

"It is. Good for you. Anything else?"

"Vitamin C, especially in the winter, when my fruit consumption decreases, and B12 when my back acts up."

"Your back?"

She explained. She'd gotten shingles—she'd thought she'd just been scratched when she'd had to negotiate her way through a dense tangle of bushes and trees to get to Tassi, who was stupidly, dangerously, challenging a raccoon, but over the weekend it got worse, not better, eventually feeling like someone had slashed her back with a knife. When she went to her doctor on the Monday, she was told it was shingles—and that she'd missed the 48-hour window during which medication would have almost guaranteed no permanent nerve damage. So now, every now and then, the nerves on the left side of her back started to tingle, but, fortunately, if she took a large dose of B12 right away, the tingling went away. And, so far, never developed into the searing pain that can apparently occur with permanent nerve damage.

"Ah. Your doctor recommended that?"

"No, I googled. And I've since been told it's common among baseball players with nerve damage in their shoulders. My doctor recommended the shingles vaccination, because you can get it twice, so I went ahead with that as well."

"Yes, good. Any other vaccinations? When was your last tetanus shot?"

"I have no idea. I went to Europe, oh, twenty years ago, and had some sort of package vaccination then, against hepatitis and some other stuff, I think. Had to get one shot, then go back, and get another. I'm now covered for life, I think."

"Probably Twinrix."

"Yes, that sounds familiar."

She looked again at the form Kat had filled out.

"You're not taking estrogen? A woman of your age?"

"No."

"But— Surely your physician recommended that you do so. There are many health benefits—"

"Actually, she didn't." It was, after all, ten years ago. When things were ... so very different.

"But every woman past menopause should be on estrogen. To compensate for the reduced production ..."

"No thank you."

The nurse made a note.

Did they interpret a refusal to take estrogen as a sign of gender dysphoria, a sign of illness?

"All right then," she put down the clipboard, "I'd like to update your tetanus and give you a broad-based antibiotic. We keep our residents pretty healthy, but living in close quarters with so many people ... we want to be proactive."

With some reluctance, aware of the spiralling downside of antibiotics, Kat gave her consent. Though, truthfully, it wasn't clear the nurse was asking for it.

"And can I keep up with the AREDS? And the vitamins?"

"Yes, I'll make a note in your file and issue you some of each. You can keep them in your room. Other meds will have to be controlled by the dispensary, you understand."

Kat nodded.

The nurse proceeded with a brief physical, pronounced her pulse and blood pressure to be excellent, took several vials of blood, gave her a couple injections, and then indicated that she was good to go.

"Feel free to make an appointment whenever you feel you need to. We don't often see seniors in as good a condition as you," she smiled, "and we want to keep you that way!"

Then let me the fuck out of here, Kat wanted to reply.

"Now, are you hungry?" Mary-Anne had been waiting for her in the outer room. "It's past dinner, but I can get you something to eat."

She hadn't eaten since … yesterday morning. She usually had half a sticky bun or a small piece of tiropita, a Greek pastry she'd discovered when she'd lived in Toronto, for breakfast. After her hike, she had some fruit, and then later some stir-fried veggies or a slice of pizza. And then a bit of snacking through the evening. Raisins in peanut butter or a handful of chocolate-covered pecans.

But she wasn't hungry. Must be the stress, she thought. The shock of it all.

"No, thanks."

"Okay, then, here's your welcome package," she handed her a thin file folder. "In it, you'll find our list of Rules and Responsibilities, which we expect you to follow. There's also a map of the facility. Meals are in the cafeteria at the stipulated times. Eventually, we hope that you'll become part of our Kitchen Team."

Not fucking likely, Kat thought. She didn't even *have* a kitchen. She had a kitchen *counter*. A sink and a fridge. She'd gotten rid of the oven to put in a doggy door. The counter held a microwave, a toaster oven, a hotplate, and a kettle. It was all she needed.

"I'll take you to your room then!"

Good. Kat wanted very much to be left alone. She'd inter-acted with more people in the last two days than she usually did in two months. This was going to be hard. Very hard.

As Mary-Anne led the way out of the infirmary, down the hall, toward the stairs, Kat followed. Tried to follow. Fell off the heels. The file folder went flying.

"Damn it!"

Mary-Anne sucked in her breath. "No swearing, please." She bent to help Kat pick up the scattered sheets.

"Well, I'm going to twist an ankle wearing these things."

"Are they the wrong size?"

"No, they're the wrong height. I told you, I've never worn heels before. I haven't mastered walking on mini-stilts."

"You've—you've *never* worn heels before?" She made another note. Then resumed leading the way.

"No, so just slow the fuck down!"

"Please, Katherine, language!"

"Don't tell me how to talk! I can use whatever language I want!" She sounded like a child. She knew it. But.

"Well, I guess you can, but you'll rack up so many demerit points, you'll never get out of here! Is that what you want?"

Kat was so busy trying to walk, Mary-Anne's words didn't quite register.

"You'll be sharing with Holly," she said pleasantly as she started up the stairs.

Oh. No.

"I don't mind being by myself," she said. Lightly. She hoped.

"But we do, I'm afraid."

Did they consider her a suicide risk? No, more likely, they thought women were supposed to be social. Maybe she could get the earplugs that had been in her waist pack. Maybe she could get herself committed to solitary. Did that happen in psychiatric institutions?

As they neared the room, her room-mate's name registered. Could Holly be *Holly*? How many people named Holly lived in North Bay? Assuming that this facility would be filled first, or mostly, with those nearest. And that Holly had moved back. They'd fallen out of touch when she'd married and moved to Ottawa. Though probably it was the marriage more than the move that had led to the dissolution of their friendship. Kat hadn't accepted Holly's invitation to the wedding. She couldn't, given her views about marriage. Simply put, as far as Kat was concerned, it was institutionalized sexism. Being a wife—well, frankly, she'd been flabbergasted when Holly had announced that she was getting married. She wasn't the type. At all. She'd thought. And since Kat thought it was a grave mistake, she couldn't possibly support it by attending the wedding. But, as Holly had pointed out, the wedding was important to her and as a friend— But if it was so important to her— Holly hadn't even introduced her to Darryl. It was all very strange.

The last time Kat had seen Holly was during a quick visit outside on the campus of the university; Kat was a sessional by then, teaching a few courses, Applied Ethics of one kind or another and Critical Thinking, and Holly was finishing up her Master's degree. She'd just gotten a dog, and Kat had wanted to meet it. (Okay, conceded, she hadn't actually *asked* to meet Darryl.) It was a delightful pup, whom Holly had jokingly said she was going to name 'Gun'. It took Kat a second, but she burst out with a laugh.

Kat had tried to maintain the friendship. But after a few weeks, her emails went unanswered. She'd been especially concerned when she'd asked Holly if she could email a completed screenplay—she'd had aspirations at the time, justified in that what she enjoyed writing most was dialogue, and was, she thought, good at it, but naïve in that getting a screenplay produced was all but impossible even if one *had* connections. She wasn't asking Holly to read it; she was just asking if she could send it in order to establish a sort of copyright—the email would be dated, so if she ever had to prove that the screenplay was hers, was written in such and such a year … Holly had refused. Why? Darryl had advised her to. Why? She didn't say.

In fact, it was Holly who'd provided the idea for the screenplay. She'd been trying to become a firefighter for years, and although she was amazingly fit, working out every day, and a very likely candidate, as she'd been a volunteer for Search and Rescue for years, she kept failing the physical test. As she'd explained, with great anger, the test favored men of a certain height and weight. First, the push-ups and sit-ups requirement. Push-ups favor bodies with a high center of gravity. For the most part, male bodies rather than female bodies. Sit-ups, on the other hand, favored bodies with a lower center of gravity. Female bodies. Applicants had to do fifty push-ups, but only thirty sit-ups. Second, the timed test for getting a folded hose off the rack and carrying it twenty feet. The rack was about five and a half feet off the ground. Shoulder height if you were over six feet tall. If you were five-four, it was over your head. Shoulder height was nice if that's where your center of gravity was. Hip height would be nice for women. Around three feet off the ground. No matter how hard Holly tried— To lift the hose off the rack and keep her balance, she'd have to stand with her feet apart and her knees bent. But then she wouldn't be able to reach it. To *reach* the hose, she'd have to stand on her tippy-toes, feet together. Which meant she'd topple over as soon as she got it off the rack. Third, running an eight-minute mile fully equipped. The smallest heavy coat was still too big, she'd told Kat. It flapped around her ankles. And the boots. It was like wearing clown shoes. So of course she kept tripping. Of course it took more than eight minutes. And climbing ten flights of stairs, let alone a ladder—so equipped— Out of the question.

All of which, Holly had pointed out, was stupid. There was no reason they couldn't put racks at different heights. No reason they couldn't make the coat and boots (and gloves) in women's sizes. And every reason *to* do that. Yes, a firefighter crew needs the brute force bodies. They could hold up the roof when it was collapsing and move the heavy stuff that had fallen on top of people. But it also needs small, yet flexible and strong, bodies to crawl under and behind, to rescue hidden and terrified kids.

Had Holly gotten pregnant? Was that the reason for the sudden and uncharacteristic decision to get married? Kat had considered the possibility. But no, that would have been even more puzzling. First, Holly would've been on contraception. Second, if the contraception had failed, she would've gotten an abortion. As far as Kat knew, Holly didn't want kids. She was so not the nurturing type.

Which was another reason Kat had lamented the loss of her friendship. Women who were mothers seemed to become … someone else. Over the years, having kids, more often than getting married, seemed the reason for Kat's shrinking social circle.

As soon as she entered the room, she saw that it was indeed Holly. Fifteen years older, of course, and not in her usual sweats and track shoes, but— Kat broke into a smile. A nervous smile.

"Holly, this is Katherine, your new roommate," Mary-Anne said.

Holly glanced at Kat, then stared, surprise and what might have been dismay, seeping across her face.

"Holly, I trust you'll provide an orientation for our new guest," Mary-Anne said cheerfully.

"Yes, of course!" Holly responded. As cheerfully. It was eerie.

"Well then, I'll leave you two girls to get acquainted!"

Both of them winced at the word.

After Mary-Anne's departure, they faced each other awkwardly. Then, after a moment's hesitation, a moment's deliberation, Holly flicked her head ever so slightly to an upper corner of the room where, Kat saw, there was a camera. Probably with a microphone.

Kat turned her glance into a full appraisal of the room. Each side was identical. A bed. A closet that was bigger than she'd need, and a desk that was smaller than she'd like. No windows. No bookcases.

"Mine?" she nodded to one of the beds. It was hard to tell because they were both made up so neatly. So unslept in. Well, not for long, that.

"Yeah."

Kat sat down heavily. Sighing, she kicked off her damned shoes. One hit the wall above her bed, the other narrowly missed Holly.

"Hey!"

"Sorry." She lay back then, rolled over, and curled into a fetal position.

"Yeah." Holly repeated. "We'll chat in the morning." Or not.

But Kat didn't fall asleep. Couldn't. Her mind was racing, trying to catch up. She was incarcerated in a psychiatric institution. For six months. Simply because she wasn't feminine. It was insane.

Okay, first things first. Her cabin. She hadn't left any appliances on, she hadn't left any windows open, the furnace wasn't on, but it wasn't winter, so the pipes wouldn't freeze … All of her bills were on automatic payment, and she had enough in her account for the next six months. And then— Hopefully *before* then, hopefully *well* before then— There had to be a way …

The door to her cabin was unlocked though. She never locked it when she went into the forest. Truth be told, she didn't lock it when she drove into town either. Her car would be in the driveway though, so things would seem— No, someone could notice that her lights never came on. But who could she call? The police? They were responsible to grabbing her off the road … On second thought, better to leave it unlocked. If anyone wanted to rob the place—though who would be interested in books and classical music?—she didn't even have a flat-screen tv yet, because as long as the old one was working—then at least they wouldn't have to break her windows. Her precious, gorgeous, five by five windows looking out at the water …

Thank god Tassi was no more. When Kat thought of what might have happened if she'd still been alive— She would've been taken to some kennel, as there was no one Kat knew who would look after her for six months, and she wouldn't have understood— She would've waited and waited, dying slowly of a broken heart, abandoned by the one she loved …

GenJen: Hey, ThinkAboutIt, I've been going through your archive—great stuff!! I especially like your piece on all the Gender Recognition Acts, back when.

    ↳ **ThinkAboutIt:** Thank you!

Youngun: What are Gender Recognition Acts?

GenJen: In the UK, The Gender Recognition Act allowed adults to officially register a change to the gender assigned at birth. But as ThinkAboutIt points out, gender isn't assigned at birth. Sex is. And you can't change sex. You can't go from XY chromosomes to XX chromosomes. You can get plastic surgery and take hormone injections, and that'll affect your secondary sexual characteristics, but that doesn't change your sex. Your secondary sexual characteristics change anyway through your life; before puberty and after menopause, males and females are more similar than they are during the 35 years in between, just half of their lives, of sexual maturity. According to the Act, applicants had to "provide psychiatric assessments and proof of living for two years in the gender they wish to be officially recognised". That doesn't make sense. Whoever wrote that must have meant sex, not gender. We've never officially recognized people for being feminine or masculine.

ExAcademe: California's Gender Recognition Act said one could request that the gender marker on a California birth certificate be listed as "male," "female," or "nonbinary." Again (and again and again), gender is not sex! And except for intersexual people, sex *is* binary. Biological fact. 'Nonbinary' refers to gender; it indicates that one prefers to be neither exclusively masculine nor feminine. And that has no place on a *birth* certificate, since one is not *born* with gender.

RiseUp: In Canada, the Canadian Human Rights Act was amended to add "gender identity or expression" as a prohibited ground of discrimination, so it became illegal to deny services, employment, accommodation, and what have you because of a person's gender identity or gender expression. At least within a federally regulated industry. And that would have been great. About time, actually. No more firing female airline attendants if they don't wear make-up, to name but one example (assuming airlines are a federally regulated industry). If only they'd interpreted the amendment correctly!!

BigRed: Yeah, it was seriously messed up.

   ↳ **LovesSarcasm:** But a shining example of international harmony!

ThinkAboutIt: Yeah, interesting phenomenon. I still haven't figured out how so many countries—half! worldwide!—so quickly adopted legislation that (1) used the wrong word, and (2) allowed people to officially change their sex, (3) just on their say so.

Word: The gender recognition acts weren't the first to make that mistake. Years prior, forms started changing, didn't you notice? Instead of asking you for your SEX, with boxes for Male and Female, they started asking for your GENDER—same two boxes. I always corrected the form.

> **LovesSarcasm:** I always wrote 'My favorite color is none of your business!'

Word: The problem (well, *a* problem) is, if gender means sex, what word do we use to refer to gender? And if we don't have a word for something ...

> **BigRed:** The same thing is happening with 'vagina'. It now means female crotch or groin. Apparently. Because I'm reading about women who shave their vagina. WTF? You do NOT want to stick a razor blade up your vagina!! Quite apart from there's NO HAIR in there!

> **Word:** Yes! And so what word do we use to refer to the tunnel to the uterus through which semen can reach our eggs and result in pregnancy? I mean, if the word for that has disappeared, then how do we get pregnant?

> **LoveSarcasm:** Immaculate conception.

> **GenJen:** It boggles the mind.

RiseUp: I think a partial explanation can be found in the desire to be tolerant. (Or at least the desire to be *seen* to be tolerant.) Respect for other people's opinions is considered a sign of maturity. In the 60s and 70s, 'we' started 'accepting' gays, lesbians, and bisexuals. After a while, transsexuals were added: LGB became LGBT.

> **Word:** A category mistake if there ever was one! 'LGB' refers to one's sexual *orientation*, to which sex one was sexually attracted to. 'T' refers to—well, that's part of the problem. A *big* part of the problem. 'Transsexual' got changed to 'transgender' somehow. Regardless, it doesn't refer to sexual orientation.

↳ **BigRed:** Weren't they initially called transvestites? Men who dressed in women's clothing. Big deal.

↳ **Word:** Yes, we also had a word for women who dressed in men's clothing: tomboys. The word has (or at least had) less stigma attached.

↳ **BigRed:** You're right! Interesting ... about the relative stigma. But it wasn't just (or completely) about dressing in men's clothing. Tomboys were simply girls who didn't embrace all the feminine shit.

↳ **Carol33:** But weren't transvestites the same? Wasn't clothing just part of it for them too?

↳ **Abby8:** I'm okay with transvestites. It's fine if a guy wants to dress in women's clothes. As Word implies, women have been dressing in men's clothes forever. I'm even okay with transsexuals—it's an extreme body modification, and can only be partial, but it's on the spectrum: tattoos and piercings on one end, bigger boobs in the middle, penis turned inside out on the other end. But transgenders? Why do we even need a word for it? I'll tell you. Because cowardly men started thinking they had to change sex in order to change gender. And because they were stupid as well, they used the word 'gender' instead of 'sex'. Or maybe because they thought of themselves as such special snowflakes, they wanted a word, a new word— 'transgender'—just for them. And they chose badly.

↳ **RiseUp:** Yes! Let's legitimize men's actions by reference to what women do! 'Bout time!

↳ **LovesScience:** I'm not okay with transsexuals. They too are using the wrong word. Since you can't change your chromosomes, you can't change your sex. So calling themselves transsexual is lying.

↳ **GenJen:** And transsexuals take hormones. That might put their body modifications onto a different spectrum.

↳ **LoveSarcasm:** The one with guys who take steroids?

↳ **Shazaam:** Transgendered men are nothing other than male tomboys. They should've just called themselves bettygirls.

↳ **Word:** Oh, I like that!

↳ **Abby8**: Except that tomboys typically don't get surgery or take hormones.

↳ **LovesScience:** Because they understand that you don't have to change your sex in order to change your gender.

↳ **OffTopic:** Remember drag queens? What were they? Transvestites? Transsexual wannabes? Transgenders? Just opportunistic homosexuals?

↳ **SeeJaneScream:** Whatever, they mocked the straightjacket of femininity those of us who are born female have to contend with, one way or another. Except they mocked, by overstatement, by exaggeration, not the straightjacket, but us. It was as if they were ridiculing us, making fun of the shit so many of us have to do to get by. As women. Not realizing that if we didn't, we'd be ostracized, not hired, sometimes fired. Their ignorance alone was an insult. It's like a white man singing Al Jolson in blackface, blissfully, shamefully, completely unaware of racism. More here[1] on the radfem analysis of drag queens.

ExAcademe: I think another explanation for the widespread embrace of transgenderism was the postmodernism fad in university programs. According to postmodernism, there is no truth. There is only *your* truth and *my* truth. We *construct* reality.

    ↳ **LovesSarcasm:** Click your heels together three times and say 'There is no gravity.'

        ↳ **RiseUp:** Yes! It's like they think how one feels is more important than any physical reality. Subjectivity trumps objectivity.

            ↳ **ExAcademe:** It's not quite that subjectivity trumps objectivity. Post-modernism says objectivity is impossible.

                ↳ **GenJen:** Either way, it's very compatible with the princess/entitled male phenomena: me, me, me, *I'm* the center of the universe.

ThinkAboutIt: Interesting comments ... But I wonder whether postmodernism created all those special little snowflakes or whether snowflakes created postmodernism.

ExAcademe: I think second-wave feminists, especially those who didn't stay in academia, forget that third-wave feminists became feminists largely because of their university studies—Women's Studies, then Gender Studies.

GenJen: Or at least have been influenced by the material in those programs.

DrWho: On that note—the post-modernism note, not the third-wave feminist note—there's been a serious decline in critical thinking. (Pity it's not a mandatory course in first year.) That's probably another reason for the blanket adoption of Gender Recognition Acts. To be critical is considered a flaw! People criticize me all the time for being judgmental.

    ↳ **LovesSarcasm:** The irony.

DrWho: Indeed. And the two are related, of course: if one is to tolerate everything, accept everything, then who *needs* critical thinking? Who needs to *know* how to judge, how to evaluate, how to determine whether X is right or wrong, whether Y is better or worse than Z …

ThinkAboutIt: And again, I wonder whether the increase in tolerance led to a decline in critical thinking or whether a decline in critical thinking led to the increase in tolerance.

SeeJaneScream: No doubt the opportunists among us—i.e., men—saw the cult of tolerance as a good thing: if everyone tolerates everything, everyone can 'get away' with everything. No doubt they also endorse the lack of critical thinking: no standards of judgment means no passing judgment. Yippee.

BigRed: I agree. This whole 'inclusive' shit is just Tolerance 2.0. What's so good about including everything and everyone? What's so wrong about excluding some things and some people?

Word: Yes! When the word 'discrimination' entered the popular vocabulary, people understood it to be negative, they thought that *all* discrimination was bad, instead of recognizing that sometimes discrimination is justified. The designated parking spaces closest to buildings for people using wheelchairs is discrimination, but few people object to them because they're justified! Classic overgeneralization, that mistaken understanding of 'discrimination'. Symptomatic of lesser minds.

Carol33: The problem with tolerance is that it doesn't discriminate, it makes no judgments. Maybe that's why it's so popular, in a world full of people *unable to make* judgements, *incapable* of *critical* thinking.

ExAcademe: And it'll take us, of course, into an amoral world, one in which there is no right or wrong, no good or bad, because everything's okay. Do you really want to live in that world? Fine. Let me hire unqualified people. Because otherwise, I'm being exclusionary.

   ↳ **LovesSarcasm:** Will you hire me to be a pilot? Because I really feel like I could be good at it.

RiseUp: But let's not forget all the irrational, emotional causes. Tolerance and post-modernism and the embrace of transgenderism became *fashionable,* even *contagious* (viral) thanks to social media. And legislators are not immune to either, emotion and social media, directly and/or indirectly.

ExAcademe: Yes, that's another thing second-wavers forget to include in their analyses. The old 'peer pressure' is nothing—*nothing*—compared to the power of social media.

GenJen: I read an article that suggested that there was a pattern in girls' schools, where they were 'transitioning' in clusters. One girl decided she was a boy and got to wear pants instead of skirts, then two or three others decided *they* were boys and so got to wear pants too.

> ↳ **LovesSarcasm:** Yeah, much better to change your sex than lobby to change the uniform.

Shazaam: And like a lot of immature people, transpeople—at least some of them—and why shouldn't they have the option of being immature, just like the rest of us—want the attention that comes when you do something extreme. It has nothing to do with gender or sex per se. Look at all the press they got back when it all started. Bruce Jenner crowned Woman of the Year. Puh-lease!

> ↳ **BigRed:** Though that might have been the 'freak factor' at work.

> > ↳ **Shazaam:** True, but restroom laws changed. For what, less than one percent of the population?

> > > ↳ **SeeJaneScream:** Less than *half* of one percent!

> ↳ **ExAcademe:** Because, as RiseUp pointed out, it's a fashion fueled by social media. And fashions fueled by social media take off more quickly and more than fashions fueled by face-to-face social interaction. Things go viral. That's the difference, the power, of social media.

> > ↳ **RiseUp:** Too bad we haven't harnessed that power for good.

⌐ **ThinkAboutIt:** Oh but we have. At least, people are working on that. Political movements. Health movements. Disease vectors. So much more is possible now. If only ...

⌐ **Word:** Yeah. If only.

---

https://www.feministcurrent.com/2014/04/25/why-has-drag-escaped-critique-from-feminists-and-the-lgbtq-community

An angry buzzing woke her up. She groaned.

"Time to get up." Holly had already turned off the alarm clock and gotten out of her bed.

"But …" It couldn't be. Time to get up.

"It's six o'clock," Holly added.

At six o'clock, Kat was usually sound asleep. Had been, in fact.

She rolled over and opened her eyes. "Hi? Good to see you?"

"Wake-up is at six. Breakfast is at eight. That gives us two hours to get ready."

"To get ready for what?"

"For … To shower, do our hair, put on our make-up, pick out an outfit …"

"You've got to be kidding."

"No." Holly sighed. "I'm not. They have a strict demerit point system here."

Again, Kat didn't quite process …

"So … can we ever go outside? Walk around a bit?"

"Yes. Between eleven and twelve in the morning, after your morning class or group at ten, and again between three and four in the afternoon, after your afternoon class or group at two."

Two hours. Well, could've been worse.

"Is there a library on site? Access to the internet?"

"Yes, sort of. And yes. Sort of. But between group therapy and your psych sessions and all the mandatory classes they'll assign to you ..."

Kat deflated at the thought of all that ... interaction.

"We have the evenings to ourselves though?"

"Yes. No, not really." Holly sighed again. "You're expected to join a quilting bee or a knitting circle or at least watch tv with the other ladies in the tv room."

Ladies? Hm. Well, she didn't actually have to *talk* to the other ladies, did she?

"So what mandatory classes are *you* assigned?"

"Quilting and knitting. They were horrified to discover that I didn't know how to do either." Holly laughed. It was a bitter laugh. "And sewing. Ditto. Flower arrangement. Interior design. Your counsellor will give you your list tomorrow. After your appointment with the beautician."

My what? Right. As if.

Kat turned over, intending to go back to sleep.

"You're not going to get ready?"

"I *am* ready," she said into her pillow. "And I'm not hungry, so I think I'll skip breakfast."

"At your peril," Holly said, bustling about. "Demerit points, remember?"

"Yeah, big wup."

"It is, actually," she paused, staring at Kat's back. Then changed her mind and left for the shower room, in her robe, carrying a towel and a small cosmetic bag that contained her soap, loofah, shampoo, toothpaste, and toothbrush.

As Kat dozed off, she thought about how Holly was ... different. Aloof. Well, she had a right to be, given what had happened between them. Maybe they could patch things up.

Though part of her felt there was more to it … In any event, Kat missed the old Holly.

About an hour later, Kat woke again. She absently rubbed at the small lump on the back of her upper arm. Tassi had developed a small lump in her left leg and fearing a tumour, Kat had made an appointment with the vet, but he'd explained that that had been the site of the rabies vaccination, it was perfectly normal—and that she should go back to her kitchen and worry about something else. Okay then.

She saw Holly standing in front of the full-length mirror that hung on the back of their door. Another thing Kat hadn't seen since she'd lived at home; her mother had had one in her room, and her sister had insisted on getting one for their room as well. She also saw that Holly's desk—oh. It wasn't a desk. It was a vanity. Aptly named. Because Holly was now sitting at it, in front of a clutter of little jars and tubes and god knows what, intently examining herself in the triptych mirror Kat had thought was a fold-up bulletin board.

"You look like you're going on a date." Kat was mildly disgusted.

Holly glanced at her in surprise, then turned back to her reflection in the mirror.

"You know," she considered her appearance, then said ambiguously, "you're right."

"But you're just going to the cafeteria, right?" Kat rubbed it in. "For breakfast?"

"Hopefully, soon, I'm going home." Holly rubbed it right back in.

"There you are!" Mary-Anne peeked into the room and saw Kat still in bed. "You little sleepyhead!"

"Don't fucking infantilize me." Kat said, without turning over. "Go ahead, make a note."

Mary-Anne almost dropped her stylish pen. "It's— I came to get you. You have your make-over today. And you're late for your first appointment."

"I don't want a make-over."

"I'm afraid it's mandatory."

"And if I don't go?"

"But— You *have* to! You'll be happy with the results, I promise!" Mary-Anne stood over her bed, robe in hand.

"Hello, Katherine!" A woman in a white lab coat greeted her at the doorway. "I'm Elena, and I'll be your esthetician today."

Kat, standing awkwardly in her lavender dress, panty hose, and heels, just nodded. She had no idea what that meant. But she followed, as the woman led her toward another room. Then stopped in the doorway and stared. It looked like something she'd seen on the cover of a new age album. *Soothing Spa* or some such. And, indeed, she heard bamboo flutes playing softly in the background. And waterfalls …

"If you'll just put this on, then come lie on the table, we'll get started."

It was nice, she had to admit a few minutes later. The music, the warmth, the sound of the water … Apparently she was in for some sort of spa treatment. Cool. She'd never gone to a spa before.

"Just close your eyes, and relax …"

She felt something warm being poured onto her leg. Massage oil? It was very pleasant. Then a towel was pressed onto the oil. Kat wasn't sure what that was all about. It quickly started to cool, and she expected the woman, Elena, to replace the towel, but instead— She ripped her skin off.

"What the FUCK!" Kat sat up, swinging. She caught Elena on her chin and several trays clattered to the floor. A few attendants came running.

"What happened?" one cried out. "Oh my god, Elena, are you okay?"

Elena was holding her jaw. "She *hit* me!"

"Because she—" Kat started to explain, but then saw the piece of fabric lying beside her. It had chunks of something stuck to it, chunks that had what looked like hair sticking out of them. She reached out to touch it. The chunks felt waxy. She looked at her leg. At the red patch of skin. They were waxing her legs?

She'd never had that done before. She'd started shaving at fifteen with shaving cream and a razor, as her mother had instructed. At eighteen, she switched to an electric razor, and at nineteen, she stopped. Convinced by the arguments of hippies and feminists. She had remained convinced.

"I'm sorry it hurt so much, but you do have a lot of hair!" Elena managed to mumble.

"Of course I have a lot of hair. I'm an adult. That's what grows on legs. Et cetera."

Wait. They weren't going to do the et cetera as well, were they?

"Well, if you can't lie still, I'm afraid we're going to have to restrain you."

"Don't think so," Kat said emphatically and started to get up off the table.

"I'm sorry, but you don't really have a choice."

Two male attendants appeared out of nowhere—no doubt someone who'd heard her scream had summoned them—and before she knew it, she was strapped to the table.

"You can't do this!" She wrestled against the straps in vain. "Get the FUCK away from me!"

"Could you please hold her in the frog position?"

The men spread her legs.

"It'll go more quickly if you'd just hold still," Elena said as she applied melted wax to her left thigh. And a moment later, ripped it off. Kat bellowed.

A few moments later, Elena paused. "Have you *never* had a bikini wax before?"

"No! I've never worn a bikini before." It was true. She'd gone straight from conservative one-piece bathing suits when she was living at home, to nothing at all once she had her cabin. In between, the few times she went swimming in a public place, she'd opted for a cropped tshirt and a pair of board shorts.

"Well, we'll have to do a trim first …"

"What? No way. NO FUCKING WAY!" She started screaming. And pulling at the restraints.

"Look, I have to say, you're being a child about this!"

"Well," she sputtered at the irrationality, "isn't that exactly what you're trying to turn me into with this prepubescent look! No leg hair, no pubic hair—"

"Don't you *want* smooth and silky skin?"

"Soft as a baby's bottom?" Kat anticipated.

Elena nodded, smiling.

"No. I want adult skin." She stared at her.

Elena held her gaze for just a moment, then turned to the attendants.

"Hold her still. I don't want to cut—"

"TAKE YOUR FUCKING HANDS OFF ME!" Kat started screaming again as the men held her legs apart.

This time, skin surely came off. She managed to get a look. Her pubis looked a little like raw meat.

"I'm sixty years old!" Kat protested. "What in god's name is the point of all this?"

"Okay, now we need to turn her over …"

Kat hoped to have a conversation with Holly at lunch, but as soon as she got close to the cafeteria, she could hear the din. She stood at the entrance, looked out at the crowd, the chaos, and decided she wasn't that hungry. She really *really* needed a cup of tea though. A whole pot if they could provide it. While she stood in line, she realized she hadn't eaten since the morning she'd been arrested and figured she'd better get *something*. Something she could take back to her room.

Apparently that was against the rules.

"But it doesn't require any cutlery," she said to the attendant who'd stopped her at the door. "It's just a cup of tea and a banana."

"Sorry, we don't allow food in the rooms."

"What about beverages? I was going to ask if I could get a little kettle, a cup, and a box of tea bags, so I could have tea in my room."

The attendant shook her head.

"Not even a chocolate bar?" She wondered if there was a tuck shop. Vending machines, at least.

"Many of our people have eating disorders …"

"Yes, but I don't."

"Sorry."

So Kat sat down, carefully, in the nearest chair, drank her tea, ate her banana, then left.

Went to her room, took off the stupid clothes, the costume, and crawled into bed. She lay on her back, legs apart. Even so, she felt herself nodding off, into a sort of stress-sleep. Must find phone, she murmured to herself. Must call lawyer.

A few minutes later, she heard Holly come in.

"You okay? You looked … hurt or something. In the cafeteria."

Kat briefly described her morning. Without moving.

"She didn't put any cream on after?" Holly asked. "It helps."

"No. She didn't. And it still hurts. Feels like the road rash I got when I crashed my bike."

"Ah. Maybe that's why she didn't put on any cream. You'll need to be careful of infection."

"How?" She turned her head to face Holly. "I mean—"

"I wouldn't wear any panties for a day or so. And definitely no pantyhose."

Oh good. She turned away to stare at the ceiling. An upside.

About an hour later, there was a knock on the door. Holly wouldn't knock, and Kat didn't want to see anyone else. So she ignored it.

Mary-Anne opened the door. Apparently residents, inmates, lost their right to privacy.

"You've got another appointment this afternoon," she said cheerily. "Now, in fact. Up you get!"

Half an hour later, having followed Mary-Anne, slowly, out of the room, down the hall, and down the stairs, she entered a room adjacent to the one she'd been in that morning and saw that it was a combination hair salon and nail salon. Not that she knew what a nail salon looked like, since she'd never been in one. It was the bottles of nail polish that gave it away. There must have been hundreds of them, sitting prettily in a dozen rack against the wall. As for ever having been in a hair salon, that had happened only twice in her life. First, when her mother had insisted that she get her hair done for her sister's wedding. And a few years later, when she wanted her long hair to be cut into a short shag. Turned out they just trimmed it. It was still easily long enough to put in a pony tail. Twenty bucks for that? So she cut it herself. She didn't end up with the feathery look she was after, but it was much closer to what she'd wanted, and within a year, she figured out how to do it well enough that if she did it on a Friday night, tweaking here and there on the Saturday and Sunday, no one stared at her in horror on the Monday.

"Good afternoon, Katherine," a woman rushed to greet her in the doorway, perhaps afraid that she'd turn and leave. A distinct possibility. "My name is Lalene, and I'll be your beautician!" She reached out and gently took her arm.

Kat grunted.

"If you'll just make yourself comfortable over here," she just as gently led her to a chair at a large sink.

A long while later—there seemed to be no end to the conditioners and thickeners and strengtheners she needed—her hair was freshly washed and turbanned. The beautician studied her face, turning her this way and that.

"We'll start with those eyebrows," Lalene said. "It looks like it's been a while."

Yeah. Forty-five years, Kat thought. At sixteen, she'd plucked her eyebrows at her mother's encouragement, but it hurt so much—a spot of blood actually appeared with every pluck—that first time was also the last time. Why did women *do* that!?

"Tilt your head back a bit?" Lalene instructed, as she leaned in with a pair of tweezers in hand.

"No, I'd prefer that you leave my eyebrows just the way they are," Kat turned her head to the side.

"Oh, I'm afraid I can't do that," she replied, leaning in again, pushing Kat's head back with surprising firmness. Quick as a snake, she plucked.

"OW!"

Kat turned her head away again. Then, as Lalene persisted, she moved it back and forth. Feeling like a four-year-old.

"Please stay still," Lalene said with frustration. "I really don't want to put out an eye!"

"Then put down the tweezers."

"Will you at least let me pluck out a few of those nose hairs?"

"No!" She'd actually done that once too, and it hurt even more than plucking her eyebrows.

"Your mustache?"

"I don't have a mustache!"

"Oh I assure you …" She held a magnifying mirror close and turned it so Kat could see.

"Well, who the fuck is going to look at me with a magnifying glass?"

"Please, watch your language."

"My language is the least of your concerns." Kat glared at her.

Lalene sat back and considered the situation. She'd never had someone this uncooperative.

"Maybe if you saw just a bit of what—"

"Get that shit away from me!" Kat knocked the mascara and eyeliner out of her hands.

"Do you know what's *in* that stuff?" she added. "Read the ingredients and google their health effects, why don't you?"

Lalene stepped away, made a call, then returned to Kat. Who, having briefly considered her options, was still there.

"Can we at least do the facial today?"

Kat gave another grunt. She had no idea what that involved.

Lalene started with a questionnaire. Kat answered 'No' to every question. Except for "How many glasses of water do you drink a day?" To which she'd replied "None."

Lalene stared at her, clearly in disbelief. "But eight glasses of water—"

"I drink about six cups of tea," Kat explained, "and sometimes a cup of hot chocolate. Otherwise, whenever I'm thirsty, some almond milk and/or juice." Kat suddenly understood why, several years ago, all of her female students had started carrying bottles of water. However inconceivable, she'd initially thought they were athletes, fresh from a workout. Then, although it happened at about the same time some institutions were worried about the quality of the water in their drinking fountains, she'd concluded it was just stupid: could they really not get through a morning or an afternoon without water? But now she knew the reason: they'd thought it was a skincare thing, a beauty thing; they were trying to drink eight glasses of water a day. Of course. Because none of her male students did it.

"You just use soap?" Lalene was horrified anew a few questions later.

"Yup."

"Since—when?"

"I don't know. Five? When does a kid start washing him or herself?"

Lalene put the questionnaire aside and began the facial.

First, she massaged something onto Kat's face. Then let it sit. Then wiped it off, then washed it off.

Then she studied Kat's skin, adjusting a very bright light this way and that, then held a magnifying glass to her face. What is it with these magnifiers? Who the fuck looks that closely at their body? At anyone *else's* body? Maybe, she thought, they used them to create the impression that what they did was dermatology, that getting a facial was science. Rocket science. Kat supposed that, despite the increasing dismissal of science, such an association would confer legitimacy. And justify exorbitant prices.

"Okay." Lalene had made a decision. "We'll do the micro-dermabrasion facial, with our own hyaluronic acid infusion."

"Whoa," Kat replied. "Don't think so." She'd been expecting a layer of green goo with cucumber slices on her eyes or some such. Silly, but hey if that's what it took to get her out of here. But abrasion? Acid?

"But it'll make your skin appear so much healthier and younger!"

"The key word there being 'appear'."

No matter. Lalene put some sort of hood over Kat, backwards, and began to steam her skin. It was like a mini sauna for her face. Or at least what Kat imagined a mini sauna for her face would feel like. She'd never had a sauna. She had to admit it felt nice. She imagined diving into the lake on a warm summer day, the water … It suddenly dawned on her. In six months, it would be too cold. She was going to miss the entire spring, summer, and fall. No. She couldn't. She survived the six months of winter *for* the spring, summer, and fall. She'd have to find a way—

Lalene turned off the steam and pulled the hood away. Kat kept her eyes closed. Thought that would help. Help her stay put. She felt Lalene smear something onto her face. Then, after a moment or so, she felt her peel it off. Kat assumed that was 'the peel' she'd mentioned. It didn't hurt as much as ripping the wax off, but she was sure some of her skin came off with the peel.

Lalene also spoke of 'skin sedation' and a 'vitalizing treatment' and a 'power mask', but Kat was convinced it was all just jargon, intended to make something simple sound complicated, something trivial sound important. She hated such verbosity. She'd gotten it from her business students every day. The verbal diarrhea that came out of their mouths always reduced to the simplest, and often ugliest, of statements. Which she demonstrated again and again. To no avail.

Lost in her thoughts, Kat lost track of the things the woman was doing to her face.

"This is a new brightening cream you're going to love," she was saying, as she began to smear something on her face. "It'll make your skin so *radiant!*"

"Hang on, what's in it? Uranium?"

"No, I don't think—" She broke off when the phone rang. "Back in a minute," she said, then thought to add, "do *not* wipe that off!"

Kat wiped it off.

"Sorry about that," she said when she returned. "Oh."

Kat tried to hide her grin.

Lalene was not amused. "That call— I've been instructed to continue with your full treatment, so we'll start with the lipstick, shall we? Save the eyes for last?"

Kat whipped her head back and forth again, as Lalene applied lipstick, and ended up with bloody smears across her face.

"Okay, maybe today we'll just— Actually, no, I don't want to do your eyeliner or your mascara when you're in this state. Even your eye shadow— Excuse me a minute."

What would they do, put her head in a vice like the guy in *Clockwork Orange*? If Lalene insisted once more, Kat decided she'd hold still. Likely lose an eye otherwise.

It turned out she didn't have to do that.

Because two attendants walked in—the same two from the day before—and before she could react, they'd applied wrist restraints to fasten her arms to the chair. Then one of them walked behind her and held her head steady.

Kat closed her eyes again. She felt Lalene slather cream on her face and scrub the lipstick off. Then she felt her slather a different kind of cream on her face. It felt a little cooler.

"If you don't open your eyes, you won't see what I'm doing."

Yeah. Rather the point.

"So how will you be able to do this yourself every morning?"

As if.

Kat kept her eyes closed. She felt something on her eyebrows. Something on her eyelids.

"Open your eyes, please."

Reluctantly, Kat opened her eyes, but kept them unfocused.

She felt something on her eyelashes.

Then something on her lips. Another something on her lips. Something *around* her lips. Good god, was there no end to this?

Something on her cheekbones.

"There!" Lalene sounded relieved. And happy with the result. "What do you think?" She held a mirror to Kat's face.

"I think I look like a clown."

"And I think you look beautiful," Lalene responded.

Well, there was no accounting for taste, Kat thought. Thank god she could wipe the whole mess off once she was back in her room.

"Now for the finale!" Lalene unwound the towel still on Kat's head.

Kat was horrified. "You *dyed* my hair?"

"Just to hide the grey," Lalene said. It wasn't as if she'd turned her into a redhead.

"I didn't give you permission to do that!" Quite apart from the chemicals, she was just fine with her grey. The rich brown she now saw in the mirror didn't match her face. Well, actually it did. Because the face she now saw in the mirror wasn't her face.

"You'll like it when we're all finished, you'll see!" Lalene dismissed her objections.

They weren't finished yet?

Apparently, Lalene had yet to cut and style Kat's hair. Fortunately, it took less than half an hour.

"What do you think?" Lalene held a mirror so Kat could see the sides and the back.

"I don't like it." She hated the pixie look she saw. "In fact, I hate it." She wanted her scruff back. She wanted her self back. She wanted her life back.

"Our nail technician will see you now."

Oh god, there was *more*?

Before she could object—not that it would have mattered— Lalene wheeled Kat over to the nail station. Debbie introduced herself then put each of Kat's hands into a little pot filled with something slick. Possibly dish detergent.

"We'll leave you soaking for a few minutes …"

Kat thought of making a run for it. But she had her heels on. Of course.

Five minutes later, five very boring minutes later, Debbie returned.

"Have you been *clipping* your nails?" she asked in horror.

No, I've been chewing them off.

She began filing each one. "Never file back and forth," she instructed. "Go from the side to the center, lifting the file each time, gently, as often as it takes to get the shape you want. And use a 240-grit file. Nothing lower."

Uh-huh.

"Be sure to hold the file flat against the nail. Otherwise, you'll thin the nail."

Uh-huh.

"And don't edge the file into the corner. That'll just encourage breakage. And we don't want that."

Oh, the horror.

Finally, she was done. With the filing. She held Kat's hand out in front of her. As if trying to figure out what shape would most flatter her hands. Which was, of course, exactly what she was trying to do.

"You've got rather square hands," Debbie said, "so I think— Actually, you've cut them so short, we don't really have anything to shape. Next time," she said cheerily. "For now though, let's get rid of the feathers …" she tucked the tip of the file under one of Kat's nails and flicked it away. Then repeated the movement for each nail.

"Now, let's see what we can do with those cuticles…" Debbie took a look, considered an array of cuticle products, then made a selection.

"This is a really good cuticle oil. It contains coconut oil and apricot oil. And lots of vitamin E, of course."

Of course.

"That'll be good for those ridges."

Uh-huh.

"All right, then, what would you like to try today?" She presented a small rack of nail polish like it was a box of bon bons.

"Bubblegum Pink? Princess Pink? Bloodred? The Scarlet Letter? Ooh, that sounds daring. I love the names they come up with."

Kat stared at her. "Do you ever *think* about the names they come up with?"

"What do you mean?"

"I mean exactly what I said. Do you ever think about the names they come up with? What they mean? What they *imply*?"

Debbie didn't reply.

Okay. Apparently not.

Half an hour later, Kat hobbled toward the door, carrying a little bag containing a nail file, the opened bottle of cuticle oil, and the opened bottle of 'To Die For' nail polish.

"Wait!" Lalene called out.

No. No more. She was done.

"I've printed out your skincare routine. And I've bundled up your scrubs, masks, and peels," she pointed at each one, nestled in a rather large silky sachet, "your cleansers, exfoliators, and moisturizers, your facial mist, your retinol, of course, and your eye creams, and finally your serums—antioxidant, clarifying, and calming."

Mutely, Kat took the bag.

"See you next week!"

What?

Kat made it back to her room, kicked off the stupid shoes—she had a blister from walking in them barefoot—and took off the stupid lavender print dress. She put on her robe, grabbed her towel and soap, and headed for the shower room. Halfway there, she turned around, went back to her room, rummaged through the silky bag looking for something labelled 'cleanser' in case soap wasn't enough to get the damn stuff off, then headed back to the shower room. Had a nice, long, hot shower. Went back to her room. Sat on her bed. What she wanted now was a long walk through the forest. A very long walk through the forest. The trees, the quiet, the solitude. The motion, simple and repetitive and rhythmic, as close, close enough, to running as she could get. She was near tears. She crawled under the covers instead.

"Katherine, are you in there?" Mary-Anne knocked on the door.

Kat groaned. "Go away!" she yelled. And felt like a teenager, sullen in her bedroom.

"I forgot to give you your class and group list. Silly me!" She'd opened the door and entered the room.

"Did I say you could come in?" Kat glared at her. "Do I have no privacy at all?"

"But— You're supposed to be attending class now. Positive Posture." She held out the list.

Kat took it and looked at it dumbly. She'd been assigned all of the classes Holly had been assigned and more. Positive Posture. There was nothing wrong with her posture. Baking with Flair, Cake Decorating, Cooking Essentials. Had Mary-Anne seen her grimace when she'd mentioned becoming part of the Kitchen Team? She'd have to give her more credit from this point on. Hair with Style and The Art of Make-up. No doubt, Lalene's suggestions. Magnificent Mothering and Great Grandmothering were unchecked. Okay, so they weren't completely insane here. But never having had kids had apparently gotten her assigned to a supplemental therapy group, Childless Women. Because *why?* Why isn't *wanting* kids just as subject to examination as *not* wanting kids? Mary-Anne had also checked off the Anger Management therapy group. Probably two minutes into the session with Elena.

"It'll help you manage your heels. The Positive Posture class."

"I doubt that."

"But— This is all— We want to help you!"

"Can you help me find a phone?" She'd remembered. Must find phone. Must call lawyer.

"Come on, up you get!"

Apparently, it was unthinkable to leave the room without her clown face on. And by the time Kat had come close, close enough, to Mary-Anne's approval, the class was over. So sad.

Kat decided to give the cafeteria another try. Maybe it would be less chaotic during dinner. It was not. She got a tray, a serving of tuna casserole and a bottle of juice, looked around for a quiet corner, then saw Holly close to the middle of the room, waving her over.

"Is it always this loud?" Kat asked once she'd made it safely to her table and was sitting comfortably across from her.

Holly nodded, smiling. "Makes it impossible for any single conversation to be heard by the ever-present microphones." She'd finished her meal and was munching on an apple.

"Ah."

Kat didn't know how to begin the conversation they needed to have. So she started in on her casserole.

"You were right," Holly said. "About marriage."

Kat looked up. A little surprised. Holly smiled. A little apologetic.

"It was like as soon as I was his wife, he expected me to act like—a wife."

"Go figure," Kat said.

Holly grinned. "Yeah, but ... I didn't think I had to be *that* kind of wife."

"I don't think there's any other kind."

"Yeah. I get that now." She took a bite of her apple. "And—"

Kat waited.

"And I think— You know we didn't really know each other before we got married. I mean we dated for less than a year."

Kat nodded.

"Anyway, he saw the tip of the iceberg in me and assumed that's all there was. I saw the tip of the iceberg in him and assumed there was more."

Kat's fork stopped on its way to her mouth. "What a perfect metaphor!" she stared at Holly with delight. "And a *huge* insight. Into the relationship between men and women."

Holly just nodded.

"How long did it last?"

"A year. A very long year."

"And then?"

"And then I was happy again."

Kat grinned.

"So how did you get here?" she asked.

"You mean 'If you can put on a wedding dress, surely you can play the femme'?"

"Actually, no, apparently I'm a couple steps, a couple *miles*, behind … everything. I didn't even think about playing the femme. Didn't know we had to."

"Which is why *you're* here."

Kat nodded.

"Search and Rescue is a manly job."

Holly saw Kat's blank look.

"You really are behind. I take it then that you still don't keep up with the news."

Kat shook her head. Holly had always been amazed that Kat didn't watch the news every evening. But it wasn't really news, Kat had explained. It was always the same old thing: competition between men presented as exciting and important, interspersed with weather reports, celebrity reports, and maybe one good deed to leave us feeling good about the world.

"They passed an amendment to the Labour Act," Holly said, "stipulating that certain jobs were to be filled by men only. For safety reasons. It was for our own good, you understand."

Kat did. Understand. Which is why she groaned.

"They didn't want women to get hurt," Holly piled it on, knowing full well.

"Right. Never seemed to affect the sexual assault conviction rate."

Holly nodded.

"But," Kat was confused, "didn't you have a government job? In the Revenue Agency?"

Holly practically spit out a chunk of apple. "How long did you think I'd last at a desk job?"

"A year?"

"A month."

"Ah." She thought it through. "Good thing you didn't get a job as a firefighter then. You might've ended up in here even sooner."

"Actually I did. Get a job as a firefighter."

Kat raised her eyebrows.

"Apparently the CPAT—the Candidate Physical Ability Test—doesn't have to be conducted with actual hoses. The Ottawa Fire Department uses weights to simulate what you have to carry."

"And the clown boots?"

"They actually *do* make fire fighting gear in women's sizes. The North Bay Department simply neglected to tell me that. Besides which, again, the *Ottawa* Department simply specifies that for the test you wear long pants, a hard hat, work gloves, and footwear with no open heel or toe."

Kat processed that. "The fuckers."

"Yeah."

"All those years you tried to pass the frickin' test—"

"Yeah."

"Have you considered suing?"

"Actually, yeah. A desk job in the government is a handy thing to have. I met someone who knew someone who knew someone … The Canadian Human Rights Act prohibits discrimination on the basis of sex. I should've known that. Should've thought of that. Anyway, I'd actually started the paperwork when—"

"The Act was repealed?" Was that also on the news she didn't watch? "Because otherwise—

"No, the amendment to the Labour Act doesn't discriminate on the basis of sex."

"Of course it does."

"No," Holly said, carefully, with a maniacal grin, "it discriminates on the basis of safety. It just so happens to align with sex." She was clearly quoting the explanation she'd been given when she'd objected.

"Ah. Okay, but," Kat was still confused, "you're here because Search and Rescue was classified—"

"I got hurt on the job. The fire fighter job."

"Oh no." She'd worked so hard to get the job. "Are you okay?" And then it hit her. "Wait a minute. Surely men get hurt on the job all the time."

"Yeah, but no one puts them on the front page. And the thing is—"

"You were hurt because someone sabotaged your equipment."

Holly nodded. They'd both seen *North Country*.

"But you didn't have proof."

Again, she nodded.

"That wasn't— That wasn't the trigger for the Amendment, was it?"

Once more, Holly nodded.

"Oh god. I'm so sorry."

"Yeah."

Holly finished her apple. Kat finished her tuna casserole.

"So a year after you got married and moved to Ottawa," Kat summarized, "you got divorced, quit your job, got a job as a firefighter, then …"

"Then quit that job when I was injured—it was just a broken leg, but I was afraid that next time it would be worse, possibly much worse—and moved back here. And started volunteering again for Search and Rescue."

"There weren't any paid positions in Search and Rescue? When it was still open to women?"

"Eventually, there was, yes. And I was hired. And then—"

"And then the Amendment was passed and— That still doesn't explain—"

"My resignation wasn't filed in time."

"You're kidding."

"Nope. Officially, I was employed by Search and Rescue when it was illegal for me to be so."

"And they arrested you? I mean you and not the Human Resources Administrator? Still, how did that land you *here?*"

"The HR Administrator said she thought I was a man. Because I was in their employ. As Search and Rescue."

"Seriously?" Kat tried to wrap her head around it. Finally managed to do so.

"And so you were arrested for Gender Fraud," she finished Holly's story, then sat back. It was insane. Then again, it was perfectly logical. If someone can be a woman just because they say they are—the whole trans fiasco, years earlier—then why can't someone be a man just because someone else says they are?

Shazaam: Someone mentioned that one of the problems with the Gender Recognition Acts is that men—men who became transwomen who claimed they were then, therefore, women—started claiming admission to women's spaces.

RadFemRocks: Yes, that's the problem radfems have with transwomen. They called themselves women. And felt entitled to invade women's spaces. Which just went to prove that they *weren't* women.

    ↳ **Word:** Not only did they claim the word 'women' for themselves, they insisted that all of us who were women start calling ourselves 'ciswomen.'

RiseUp: MichFest closed down because of that. They totally ruined it. They also demanded—demanded—that they be allowed to use women's restrooms, that they be sentenced to women's prisons rather than men's prisons, that they be hired to work at women's shelters.

    ↳ **Youngun:** What's MichFest?

        ↳ **BigRed:** Google it! Educate yourself about women's history! Call yourself a feminist?

Shazaam: Yeah, okay, thanks, but I was just going to point out that they also ruined women's sports.

GenJen: Technically, that wasn't necessarily transwomen. Back in 2015, the Olympics Committee said that any male could compete in any women's event as long as his testosterone levels were, for a year, in the lower range of typical male levels. They didn't have to go through a legal gender change. They didn't have to have undergo any trans medical treatment. I suppose, technically, they didn't even have claim to be women.

Shazaam: Really? I didn't know that!

LovesScience: But typically they *did* claim to be women, didn't they? So the sports world defines 'woman' by hormone level? But that's wrong. Our DNA is what determines our sex. XX or XY or some anomalous variation thereof.

    ⌐ **GenJen:** Well, at least it's a step up from using make-up and clothing as the measure. Which is what so many transwomen seem to do.

        ⌐ **BigRed:** And/or surgery. Which can only be cosmetic. Superficial.

        ⌐ **RadFemRocks:** Let alone a lifetime lived *as a female* (in a male supremacist society).

Word: The lack of a precise definition—or rather, the inability of lesser minds to establish or understand a precise definition—might have been exactly the reason for getting on the self-identity bandwagon.

DrWho: And of course the problem with self-identity is the problem with any self-report: if that's all there is, it's unverifiable.

ThinkAboutIt: And our legislators passed laws on the basis of such!

SeeJaneScream: It really is ridiculous, the notion of self-identity. As someone on FC suggested, adults could identify as children and compete in kids' competitions. (And the kids, well, they'd just have to try harder if they want to win.)

⌐ **GenJen:** Yes! She also mentioned that able-bodied people could identify as disabled and compete in the Special Olympics.

⌐ **LovesSarcasm:** No, wasn't it wheelchair basketball? That would be so hilarious. A bunch of guys running around, claiming to be disabled, playing in a wheelchair basketball game... Very Monty Python.

Abby8: But we *didn't* see men flooding the women's events, as a result of the Olympics Committee decision.

⌐ **BigRed:** Maybe because most male athletes are in the mid and upper range of testosterone.

⌐ **RadFemRocks:** And because most men would find it emasculating to compete with women. To win over a woman doesn't have much status among men.

⌐ **SeeJaneScream:** Because they don't consider us worthy opponents.

⌐ **RadFemRocks:** Exactly.

Shazaam: Do the regulations also allow any female to compete in any men's events as long as her estrogen levels are in the lower range of typical female levels for a year?

Abby8: No, wouldn't that have to be as long as her testosterone levels are in the higher range of typical female levels?

Dick: Doesn't matter. They'd lose anyway.

 ↳ **RadFemRocks:** Perhaps, but not because they're not as good, per se. Rather, because almost all sports are defined, measured, by male standards. By, typically, brute muscular strength, especially upper body muscular strength. Imagine sports redefined, measured, by, say muscular flexibility. Imagine, for example, a men's balance beam event. If women were allowed to compete in *that* event, we'd wipe the floor with them.

 ↳ **Shazaam:** You're right! Ditto all so-called rhythmic gymnastics events. Better named coordination and artistic events. Men haven't even *dared* to compete in events they *know* we're better at.

 ↳ **RadFemRocks:** Which explains why there *isn't* a men's balance beam event. Or men's rhythmic gymnastics. Read Colette Dowling's *The Frailty Myth*.

 ↳ **SeeJaneScream:** They're such fuckin' cowards.

 ↳ **BigRed:** I'd love to see a men's synchronized swimming team. They'd drown each other before they'd cooperate with each other. Men synchronizing themselves? Never happen.

 ↳ **LovesSarcasm:** Well, unless we gave 'em guns. Soldiers. 'Course, they'd still end up killing each other.

 ↳ **SeeJaneScream:** Yeah. Let's do that then.

Youngun: So what did you all do, back then, advocate for a separate category for cis-women?

RadFemRocks: No! *They* should have advocated for a separate category for *trans*-women!

BigRed: What happened was women started doing it too. Claiming to be men and demanding access to *men's* spaces.

GenJen: To men's sports, no less. The Holy Grail.

BigRed: Exactly. And that's when the shit *really* hit the fan.

Youngun: What do you mean?

RiseUp: Oh clueless one, get thee to a library! Women started self-identifying as men to compete in men's sports and a few of them beat their male competitors and all hell broke loose.   NO NO NO!   NOT ALLOWED!   CAN'T HAVE THAT!

↳ **Dick:** You mean a few got lucky.

↳ **BigRed:** Luck had nothing to do with it. When we beat them in wrestling, it was because women typically have better coordination, speed, reflex, and strategy; brute force of muscle isn't the only important factor. Boxing? Women are faster on their feet; we're way better dancers. Distance swimming? Women have greater buoyancy. The biathlon? Skiing is more technique than strength and shooting is all about hand/eye coordination. Diving? No problem to compete with men. Ditto archery. Distance running? About twenty-five percent of the women who run a marathon can finish in under four hours, thereby beating about sixty-five percent of the men who run. Gymnastics. Women have always been better in the floor event. More artistry—most men can't move to music very well—and just as impressive tumbling runs because they're smaller, more compact, a known advantage for tumbling.

⤷ **Dick:** Yeah, no fair!

⤷ **BigRed:** And the high bar? Because of their lower center of gravity, women developed a whole new style that was far more interesting to watch, far more aesthically pleasing.

⤷ **LovesSarcasm:** Piece of cake, really. Only one bar to worry about.

⤷ **SeeJaneScream:** Remember that one guy? Who insisted on competing on the unevens?

Word: YES! Remember the rhetoric? 'We need to protect our boys!'

⤷ **LovesSarcasm:** Our girls? Not so much.

BigRed: Yes, protect them from the shame! A man would rather die than be beaten by a woman.

⤷ **RadFemRocks:** Which is what actually happened.

⤷ **Youngun:** What? Some guy killed himself when a woman beat him?

⤷ **LovesSarcasm:** Why didn't we think of this? Before?

SeeJaneScream: Which just piled on the insult. To women. Implying, as it does, that we are inferior to them. Otherwise, why would it be particularly shameful for a man to be beaten by a woman?

BigRed: But the thing we have to remember is that even with the impressive showing of women competing against men, in many sports, they *are* less *apt* to win. And winning can mean scholarships, endorsements, sponsorships.

ExAcademe: Good point. We also have to remember that *that* started even *before* the Olympics Committee made the change. Both the Department of Justice and the Department of Education consider a student's gender identity as the student's sex for purposes of Title IX and its implementing regulations.

    ↳ **Carol33:** Title IX is an American thing, right?

        ↳ **ExAcademe:** Yes. "No person in the United States shall, on the basis of sex, be excluded from participation in, be denied the benefits of, or be subjected to discrimination under any education program or activity receiving Federal financial assistance."

RiseUp: You'd think that at least the Department of *Education* would get it right. The gender-isn't-sex thing.

    ↳ **LovesSarcasm:** Why would you think that?

GenJen: Maybe it's time for all sports to be desegregated by sex and segregated instead by whatever feature is most relevant. Just as, at the moment, wrestling is segregated by weight and marathon running by age.

BigRed: In addition to sex.

GenJen: Right, but we can use those as precedents. For segregation by features *other than* sex. We could add things like, I don't know, foot size for sprint swimming? Because the larger your flippers, the faster you'll be? Percentage of body fat for long distance swimming because that increases buoyancy and makes it so much easier.

DrWho: But isn't, wasn't, the testosterone standard a step in that direction?

GenJen: It might have been if they'd established, say, five levels of testosterone and a competition category for each one.

   ↳ **Shazaam:** And added estrogen levels. I know for a fact I'm a better runner at certain times in my cycle.

      ↳ **Abby8:** Yeah, I've always thought they should do a study to see if there's a correlation between, say, Olympic medal winners and their cycles.

         ↳ **Shazaam:** Except that at that level, most women have stopped menstruating.

      ↳ **Abby8:** Might still have varying estrogen levels though?

Word: And if they'd taken 'male' and 'female' and 'man' and 'woman' out of the rulebook altogether.

Kat was scheduled to see her psychiatrist the next day. Actually, she'd been scheduled to see him on Fridays, three days later, but Mary-Anne had informed her that they'd been able to move it earlier. Given.

Given?

She found the psychiatrist offices on the second floor, introduced herself to the receptionist, then sat in the outer room to wait. Curious. She'd never seen a psychiatrist before. Nervous. About the power his, or her, most likely his, judgment would have over her.

"Can you tell me where the phones are?" she thought to ask the receptionist. "For resident use?"

"Sure. First floor, just outside the admin offices."

"Thanks." She thought it odd that she hadn't noticed them if that's where they were. Must be the stress.

She glanced at the magazines on the low table in front of her. *Cosmopolitan, Vogue, Good Housekeeping, Better Homes and Gardens.* They were really pouring it on. Then again, she realized, those were exactly the magazines every doctor's office would have. And every dentist's office. Every government office … Except they'd also have *Car and Driver, Popular Mechanics* … She wondered then where the male patients were. A separate wing? A separate facility? There must be some …

"The doctor will see you now," the receptionist nodded to an office with a now-open door.

"Thanks." Kat got up and entered the office.

"Hello Katherine, I'm Dr. Gagnon," he looked up from his desk, and smiled. "Please have a seat."

Okay. So far, so good. Very business-like. She didn't want touchy-feely. She sat in the chair across from his desk. The beard was a point against though. Over-differentiation. Over-compensation.

"I understand you were quite violent yesterday," he leaned back. Oh. That was the given. "We can't have that." He looked at her sternly.

We can't have that? Another point against. It was so patronizing. The phrasing, the tone, the attitude … This was not going to work.

"Does involuntary commitment permit assault causing bodily harm?" she asked.

"Oh I'm sure you're exaggerating," he smiled again.

She ignored the smile. Had to. "What's the definition of assault? And bodily harm?"

"No doubt they were just trying to help." He ignored her questions. So not going to work.

"And parents who hit their kids are just trying to teach them a lesson. And guys who rape are just trying to have a little fun. Intent might mitigate. *Might*. It does not justify, let alone excuse."

He stared at her. A bit open-mouthed.

"I understand you're angry," he recovered. "But—"

"Damn right, I'm angry! Is that a problem?" Of course it was a problem. "I shouldn't even *be* here! I wasn't given the chance to object, to explain—"

"All right, let's go over the evidence," he said kindly, nodding to a report that lay in front of him.

But she wasn't looking for kindness.

"You can tell *me* your objections, your explanations." He picked up the report then and read from the top of a list. "One, no make-up."

Oh god, this was going to take forever.

"I don't like the way it feels. I don't like the way it looks. And I especially don't like that it endorses the preference, the expectation, that women look beautiful and young. Not to mention its endorsement of the extreme importance of women's appearance."

"No jewelry."

"I don't like things hanging around my neck or around my wrists. You know the history, right? Shackles? Slavery? And things dangling from my ears is downright dangerous. Clip-ons pinch, and I'd rather not have any part of my body pierced. And, again, the practice, the custom, endorses the notion that women are to be adorned, are to be objects of beauty. That said, I do consider some jewelry aesthetically pleasing and do not object to hanging crystals in my window, for example."

He nodded, then continued. "No dresses, skirts, blouses, leggings. No heels."

She explained the discomfort. The reduced freedom of movement.

"Men's clothing."

"I don't—okay, yes, my socks come from the men's department. Women's socks are generally too thin to be warm enough; also the thickness of men's socks gives me more cushioning. I could buy good women's socks in specialized sports stores, the ones that carry hiking stuff, but they'd be way more expensive than the men's work socks you can get in department stores.

"My t-shirts are also usually from the men's department: women's tshirts have tight little sleeves—I don't like the way they cling; they also go in at the waist, and again, I prefer my clothing to have a little room.

"And sometimes my sweatshirts are from the men's department, depending on the colour. You can't get fuchsia in the men's department." There. Let him ruminate about that. "That's my favourite color. It's a sort of deep pink," she rubbed it in.

"But it's not like I wear men's underwear. Or a jock strap. I'm fully aware that my body is female."

"Your students report that you used to wear a men's suitcoat."

"Yes—" Wait, he had access to … her students? From— Fifteen years ago?

"It had pockets for my wallet, my keys, etc.," she explained. "Which I prefer to have on me instead of in my knapsack. And again, I prefer the straight up and down cut; it's far more comfortable. Have you ever worn women's clothing?"

He laughed.

"What's so funny about that?"

He couldn't say.

Neither could she. There was more to it than the surprise at thwarted expectation, the standard incongruity theory of humor. It involved, somehow, the inverted hierarchy. But why that was funny escaped her.

"And yet, you've had top surgery!" he said, apparently returning to her insistence that she wasn't confused about her body.

"I had a bilateral mastectomy," she clarified. "It was a pre-emptive strike against cancer. Stage zero."

"Stage zero? I've never heard of that." He said it in a way that suggested she was making it up.

She raised her eyebrows. Just how educated was he?

"The diagnosis was DCIS—ductal carcinoma in situ. That's when abnormal cells are found in the ducts. It's stage zero if they haven't yet spread into the surrounding tissue."

"Still, isn't removing the entire breast a little extreme?"

"If necrotizing fasciitis developed in my leg and there was a chance it could spread to the rest of me, I'd amputate in a second. Wouldn't you?"

He didn't reply. But of course he would.

"And I didn't even *like* my breasts."

She knew it the minute she said it—

"And why is that?"

"I was a runner. Figure it out."

She waited.

"Even so," he protested, "I would think that a real woman would value her breasts much more than you obviously did."

She ignored, for the moment, his reference to being a 'real' woman.

"I value my life even more. It was minor surgery. If it had progressed—"

"But you also had yourself sterilized at—" he consulted another report, "at age thirty! You were in your prime child-bearing years!"

"Exactly. And I didn't want to bear a child. But I *did* want to have sexual intercourse. Ergo."

He just stared at her.

"What was the point in waiting until I was forty?" she asked, elaborating. "I should have done it at twenty and saved my body ten years of being on the pill."

"But again, isn't sterilization a little extreme?"

"Do you know what being on the pill does to you? Nausea, headaches, and increased risk of blood clots, thrombosis, heart attack, stroke."

"Well, what about a patch? An implant? An IUD? Condoms? You had other options."

"Patches, implants, and hormonal IUDs have the same side-effects as the pill," she said, horrified at his ignorance.

"And copper IUDs also cause nausea and headaches, as well as allergic reactions, backaches, pelvic pain, and uterine perforation.

"And condoms break. And, although this was after my time, haven't you ever heard of stealthing?"

Again, he ignored her question.

"But don't you see? You obviously didn't, don't, value your womanhood."

"My what?" She burst out laughing.

Oh no. Do not laugh at a man. Especially when that man—

"Your capacity to bear children!" he said angrily.

"You're right. I don't value that. I value my capacity to be a writer. A teacher. A philosopher."

And again, as soon as she said it—

"Yes, on that note, you will agree that Philosophy is a male discipline. Logic."

She snorted. "Logic is all about relationships. Between premise—evidence, reasoning—and conclusion. So ... a *male* discipline? Don't think so."

"Yes, I note that you never married. Can you explain *that?*"

"Why should I have to? Do you ask married women to explain *their* choice?"

"Well, surely it goes without saying."

"No, it doesn't. Why does a woman voluntarily enter into a legal contract with a man, especially a contract that obligates her, in the event they divorce, to give him half of whatever she had *before* they married *as well as* a percentage of her future income?"

Given that, she didn't understand why men married either. Unless it was for unlimited sexual access. Presumed.

"So you don't want a man to look after you, to care for you—"

She snorted again.

"To provide for you financially."

Did he not hear what she'd just said?

"No. I can look after myself," she said. Fully aware of the irony. "I value autonomy. Maturity."

"Well, then," he closed her file, "you'll appreciate, and cooperate with, our work, the work you and I will do, to reach an understanding of the consequences of your actions." There was threat and reprimand in his tone.

"I think—" She reconsidered. And wisely shut up.

"All right, then," he stood up. "That's our time for today, but next week I'd like to discuss your diagnosis."

"As would I."

He looked at her. What, surprised she could handle such a grammatical construction?

"I'll give you some literature to read in the meantime. Perhaps that'll give us a jumping off point, yes?"

"Okay."

"And I'd like you to think about your gender identity."

"My what?"

He just smiled. As if she hadn't been seriously asking what he meant.

She ventured into the cafeteria for lunch and was happy to see that Holly had saved a chair for her. There was a lot she wanted to ask her.

"Hey, how's it going?" Kat set her tray onto the table. A cup of tea, a bottle of juice, and a pear.

"Oh well, you know. Actually, you don't, yet, but."

"So … you said we have access to the internet, yeah?" She tested the temperature of her tea. "It'd be nice if I could keep working while I'm here."

"You're not still teaching at Nipissing?"

"No, left that years ago."

"But you loved teaching!"

"I did. But more and more what I was doing was managing hostility. Male students in particular seemed to resent my expertise. And so could not, would not, learn from me."

Holly nodded.

"For the last ten years or so, I've been working for a company in Princeton, the one that does the GRE. I write some of the reasoning questions that go on it."

"Ah. You might want to rethink that."

"What do you mean?"

"Well, if they find out …"

Apparently any job that required a graduate degree was inappropriate for a woman. The graduate degree itself was inappropriate. So Kat decided to keep quiet about writing for the GRE. Though wouldn't they already know? Given everything else her psychiatrist already knew?

"Could I at least send them an email? Let them know I'm not available for … a while? I don't want to be out of a job when this is all over."

She took a long sip of her tea. Maybe she could tell her contact at ETS what had happened. Maybe they could get her out. It was a stretch. And—wait—did she *want* them to know? Unjustified or not, being in a psychiatric institution carried a stigma. They'd never consider her to be quite as competent again.

Besides, surely people already knew. About what was happening. Surely someone was already trying to ... what? Get the law repealed? That could take a long time.

Too, why would she think Princeton— Actually, the company wasn't affiliated with the university, but even if it was— It was at Yale that the men had famously chanted 'No means Yes, Yes means Anal!' That had been such a ... not a betrayal, or not *only* a betrayal, but the final damning bit of evidence— If an institution with such status, an institution held up as an *examplar*— And an *educational* institution at that. Yale had accepted, had *taught*, the men who'd happily chanted such misogyny, such blatant disregard for women's autonomy, their personhood, their *humanity*.

"It's ETS, right?" Holly asked. "The company?"

"Yeah."

"Well, they might not recognize it. If you keep your message short and vague ..."

"You mean they *read* our outgoing emails?"

"Probably."

"Hm." Kat thought about that as she finished her tea. She got up to get another cup. She wasn't really hungry, so she thought maybe she could smuggle out the juice and pear for later. No, wait, the damned dress had no pockets.

"Try swinging your feet forward," Holly suggested when she returned, "instead of lifting them."

"What? Oh. Okay." She set her tea safely onto the table, then ventured a lap around the table. Did as Holly suggested. Caught a heel on the floor—broke it off, actually—and went sprawling.

"Fuck."

Holly waited, grinning, while Kat smashed the other shoe onto the floor again and again and again until its heel came off as well. Then she calmly got up, slipped both shoes back onto her feet, and walked the few steps back to her chair.

"You're right," she said. "That *is* better."

Holly exploded with laughter.

"So," Kat waited until she was done, happy to see the old Holly back, at least for a minute, "you're here for Gender Fraud too, yeah?"

Holly nodded. "And Gender Dysphoria. They add that after your first session with your psychiatrist. It's sort of included with Gender Fraud, but a Judge can't make that determination."

"But he already did. In having me committed. Instead of imprisoned."

"Yes, but technically—"

"Six months?"

Holly nodded again.

"So, what, we just have to stay the course for six months and we're out of here?" That shouldn't be *too* hard. She took a sip of her tea.

"Six months *renewable.*"

"What?" Kat's hand shook a little as she set down her cup of tea. "What do you mean?"

"After the six months, your psychiatrist can file a CR. A Certificate of Renewal. Essentially it becomes a CIA. A Certificate of Involuntary Admission."

"They can do that?"

Holly nodded yet again. "Under the Mental Health Act. Section 20. They can issue a renewal 'If he or she—your psychiatrist—is of the opinion that the patient has previously received treatment for a mental disorder of an ongoing or recurring nature that,'" she clearly had it memorized, "'when not treated, is of a nature or quality that likely will result in serious bodily harm to the person or to another person, or substantial mental or physical deterioration of the person, or serious physical impairment of the person.' The second one is where they get you. Us. 'Substantial mental deterioration.'"

Right. That could be interpreted to mean almost anything.

Never mind that it was the six months that was likely to cause said substantial mental deterioration. Not the supposed gender dysphoria.

Next day, she went looking for Mary-Anne to ask about the nurse's shoes. Or something. Although her de-heeled high heels were an improvement, there was still no cushioning, and she'd already experienced the screaming nerve thing several times.

In addition, after just three days, she'd started worrying about the effect of the clothes she had to wear. An orange jumpsuit, though comfortable, would have been disturbing enough. Its purpose was not only easy identification, should an inmate escape, but also depersonalization. And stripping someone of their individual identity was an important step in reconstructing their identity. Should the goal of prison include rehabilitation.

But this—having to wear a dress, and pantyhose, and heels—it was very disconcerting. It not only stripped her of her chosen identity, it replaced it with something so foreign, so *objectionable*— She felt simultaneously infantilized and sexualized. Were they consciously doing that? Or were they just perpetuating convention?

And not being able to do all the things she used to do— Read, write, listen to music, go for long walks in the forest, go out on the lake in her kayak— Even without Tassi by her side, the forest, the lake— She felt her *self* slipping away. Her resistance, her strength, her power …

She also started worrying about her lack of appetite. When she'd been picked up, she already weighed less than what she'd weighed in her 30s, less than what she'd weighed in her 20s— she'd been at her teenage weight. She couldn't afford to lose any more.

"Katherine!"

Kat turned around. And there she was. Mary-Anne.

"I was just coming to find— You're wearing the same dress! You had it on yesterday too, as I recall. Never the same two days in a row, let alone three!"

"What? But—"

"And aren't you supposed to be in one of your classes? You realize that skipping class is on the demerit points list, right?"

"Yes, well … Remember we spoke about shoes? Well, I'd like to walk outside every day. When we're allowed to. And having walking shoes would enable me to get the most out of the exercise. Put a bit of colour in my cheeks and a smile on my face! Probably improve my posture, to boot!" Was she good or what?

"I see."

"And I wonder if I could have some earplugs. I find the noise in the cafeteria so loud … I'm not used to such an overload. And unfortunately Holly snores sometimes. Or maybe it's me. Either way, I'm not sleeping well."

"I see."

"An eyething would be nice too." She didn't know what they were really called. A two-eyed pirate patch? "To make it completely dark. At night. So I can sleep."

"Well, you could check the boutique, but I suggest you talk to your psychiatrist about your trouble sleeping. And your 'overload' problem, as you phrased it."

"I didn't phrase it as a problem. I just said … I don't like— I'm not used to living in such close quarters with so many people."

"I see."

Damn. She should have stopped after the shoes. Then she caught up. "The boutique?"

"Yes, most of our patients have friends and relatives who bring them things on visiting day, but we also have some supplies available here on-site. You didn't see them when you went to pick out your wardrobe? It's mentioned in your orientation package. You may find shoes more to your liking there as well."

Pick out her wardrobe?

"Oh, right." She'd kept forgetting to read the orientation package. That was not like her. "Okay, thanks."

"Down the hall and to your left," Mary-Anne called out helpfully as Kat left. Saving her an agonizing trip back up to her room.

Despite its name, 'The Boutique'—actually 'La Boutique'—looked like a Stedmans. One of those pre-Walmart everything stores. Kat wandered around. One aisle, 'Health and Beauty'—why were the two combined? It hadn't occurred to her before. But yes, every drug store had a substantial collection of cosmetics. Which made it seem like wearing make-up was a good thing, a *healthy* thing, like all those products were actually *good* for your skin and hair ... She found earplugs and an eyething—a 'Beauty Mask'. Right. Because the only value of a good night's sleep is to make you look good. And, in the same aisle, essentials like toothbrushes, toothpaste, and regular soap. Hm. Was that a test? Would she get a demerit point if she got a bar of soap instead of one of the cleansers?

Another aisle contained, inexplicably, kitchen things.

Clothing took up two aisles. There were miniskirts—seriously?—and what were they called ... pencil skirts. May as well wear a straightjacket. She recalled dresses with zippers up the back. (Yes, let's make it impossible for a woman to even dress herself without help.) Perhaps the similarity was the point. But was it understood to be cause or effect?

She flipped through the collection, stopping at a long, ankle-length dress. Hm. She looked at the tag. It was a 2XL. Which surprised her. But it shouldn't've, because surely they'd have to provide *some* large clothing. It was frilly and peach-coloured, but … She took it off the rack. Then added the only other long dress she saw, as well as a multi-coloured long skirt … a peasant skirt.

"Is there somewhere I can try these on?" she asked the attendant.

"Fitting rooms are at the back."

The peach-coloured dress was shapeless. Perfect. The silky navy one had a plunging neckline. But if she wore a tshirt underneath … She couldn't button the peasant skirt, but if she could move the button …

She browsed a bit more and found some tshirts, one an XL, and, much to her delight, knee socks! She could wear *them* underneath. No more panty hose! And no more waxing sessions. Not that she'd intended to keep her body hairless anyway. But at least now, no one would stare at her. Or make a note.

Shoes … Again, she lucked out. Among the many high heeled shoes, there was a pair of white nursing shoes. With thick crepe soles. Perfect. Oh. Size 7. Well, she could cut the toe out. No wait, there was another pair. Hm. Size 9. She decided better to go too big. She could double up on the socks. It would add even more cushioning. Sitting beside the socks—she'd taken six pair—were the undergarments. She'd wear nothing at all before she'd wear any of the thongs on display. Men had rejected the tight, tiny, and revealing 'speedos' (and thank god they had); why hadn't women done the same? She moved on. Wait—girdles? When had they come back? The labels identified them as 'spanx'. Seriously? As in 'spanks'? What the fuck.

She remembered to look for a sewing section, found it, and selected a spool of thread, and … no buttons big enough to fit the hole in the peasant skirt. Ah—something better! Two-inch wide elastic. No needles though. Right. Probably no knives in the kitchen section either. Well, maybe she could make the adjustment in sewing class.

The attendant scanned her items before she left. Probably just inventory control, Kat thought to herself, but then again, maybe Mary-Anne would be informed— She didn't care. She really just—didn't care.

When she got back to her room, she realized it was almost eleven. She'd totally missed her morning class. Such a pity. Happily, she changed into her new clothes—she'd changed her shoes as soon as she'd left the boutique—then headed outside. Practically ran. For the full hour, she walked around and around the—well, it was bigger than a courtyard, not big enough to be called the grounds, and too well-kept to be called a field. She'd call it a yard.

As she was walking, it occurred to her that if she could get the Gender Dysphoria charge dismissed, she could get transferred to a prison. She could serve a sentence, with no extensions, for Gender Fraud. She might even be able to get out early for good behaviour.

But did she really want to be in a prison instead of here? She knew about Zimbardo. She'd seen the trailer for that new tv series. Yeah, but that was tv. They glorified, exaggerated, the violence. And maybe women's prisons were different. She remembered reading somewhere that most women were in prison for justified violence against men. The experience might actually be interesting. There'd be the boredom, the routine, the no long afternoon hikes, but that was the case here too.

Maybe she could even get the Gender Fraud charge dismissed.

Failing that, if she could prove she wasn't a danger to herself or to others even though she presumably had Gender Dysphoria … Because that's what justified the involuntary commitment, the danger, right?

No, Holly had said it was the 'serious mental deterioration' issue, not the 'danger to' issue. The stress must be getting to her. Already she wasn't thinking clearly.

So maybe she should wait and see. Or wait until the six months were up. If her psychiatrist *didn't* renew her order, she'd be home free. Home. Free.

On her way to the cafeteria for lunch, she found the phones and called Cynthia. She needed to discuss her options, see what her lawyer thought she could do. She left a message.

"Not a word about my fashion sense," Kat warned, as she sat down across from Holly, an egg salad sandwich, an apple, and a cup of tea on her tray.

Holly looked at her. And nodded. "There are no words for your fashion sense."

"You know they'll charge you, right? I saw the navy silk on your bed," Holly explained, as she took a bite from her own egg salad sandwich. "They put it on your account and you have to pay. When you leave."

"Really?" Kat looked at her. "How do they figure that? They're forcing us to be here—"

"We're here because of something we did. Consequences."

Kat snorted. "Are they also going to charge us room and board?"

Holly nodded.

"Seriously?" She'd been joking.

Kat thought about that while she finished her sandwich. Well, it would be money well-spent, what more could she say?

"So who's your lawyer?"

"Been there, done that."

"What do you mean?"

"You want to file an appeal, right? Dispute the charges."

"Well, yeah."

"Tried that. Don't waste your time. Or your money."

"Really?"

Holly nodded.

Hm. Maybe Cynthia Seder was a better lawyer than the one Holly had. And if not, maybe she could *get* a better lawyer.

"So *who's* your lawyer?"

After lunch, she called her lawyer again, this time arranging a call-back time—two weeks hence. Plus three days.

Next day, she went to the library, hoping to get online, but there were only so many computers and everyone wanted to get online, so you had to sign up for a time slot. A time slot of fifteen minutes. The next available time slot was several days hence.

She looked in vain for legal information. The nonfiction section was small, and limited, apparently, to what they used to call home-ec.

The fiction section was dominated by women's fiction and chick lit. That is to say, romance. Not a new problem, that. Who even came up with 'women's fiction' and 'chick lit'? And why?

If she could get a laptop, or even a pad of paper and a pen— she hadn't seen either at La Boutique—she could work on her own book. It was a novel about two women who meet at a televised debate about science and religion; the one challenges the other to jump out of a plane with her; she'd wear a parachute, because gravity, and she suggested that the other woman not, because faith.

"Are there any laptops available for loan?" Kat inquired at the desk. Back before every student had their own touchpad, the university library had a collection of laptops for the less-advantaged students to use on occasion. So she thought, she hoped—

"Sorry, no."

"Can I get a pad of paper? A pen?"

"What would you need a whole pad of paper for?"

Now that she had a pair of decent shoes, she went outside to walk around and around the yard every morning and again every afternoon. Rain or shine, as they say.

Otherwise, she spent a lot of time in her room. Partly to be alone, to get away from all the people. And partly because it was the only time she could take off the damn clothes. Her new outfits were far more comfortable than the one Mary-Anne had picked out for her, but still. It was … disconcerting. It was turning her into something, someone, she wasn't. Distancing her from who she was.

Occasionally she read, some awful book from the library. And wrote a scathing review in her head.

Otherwise, like the guy in *Shawshank*, she listened to all the music that was in her head. Most often Pachelbel. With loons in the background.

At the beginning of the second week, she decided to go to the assigned Cake Decorating class. Mainly out of boredom. It was, as she expected, straight out of the 1950s. Or, rather, the early 70s, since, at least at her school, it took until she was in grade eleven for girls to be allowed to take Shop instead of Home-Ec. She'd been one of the first to sign up. A year later, when the school converted a classroom in the basement into a weight room, she and Joan started using it. They were on the field hockey team, the track team, and the gymnastics team, and although there wasn't actually a rule that said the new weight room was for boys only, that was clearly the understanding. But when Mr. Gerard found them there, he just grunted; he knew better than to tell them they had to leave.

And now— What *happened* to the 60s and 70s? Men had worn their hair long in the 60s. They'd become kind and sensitive. Cat Stevens, Harry Chapin, Dan Hill ... Women had stopped wearing make-up, they'd stopped shaving, they had access to the pill and so could have sex without the fear of pregnancy, they'd stopped getting married... It was called Women's Lib, not feminism, because all of those changes were indeed liberating. It was an era of trailblazers. By the end of the decade, we had not just contraception, but abortion, marathon runners, ivy league students ...

What the hell happened? Was it all just a fad? To those of her generation who eventually gained power? That is, the men? Because, yes, Stokeley Carmichael. The only position for women in the movement is prone.

Well fuck you, so many women had said.

Where were they now?

She looked around her. The room was full of women, several sitting at her table, but every one of them was looking at the flat rectangular cakes sitting in from of them.

Sighing, Kat did likewise. The cake was already iced in white. Probably someone's achievement in Baking class. She looked at the little tubes of frosting sitting in a Tupperware container to her right. Whatever she did with the cake, it wouldn't have any depth. The colors she had to work with couldn't provide depth. There were no shades, no tints ... A mediocre artist could achieve more depth working on a two-dimensional canvas than she could achieve working on a three-dimensional cake. Hm. Maybe if she decorated it with a path into a forest, if she made the path smaller and smaller as it wound toward the distance, achieving depth with perspective ...

She rummaged in the cupboards, found the icing sugar, some margarine, some food coloring, and went about making several shades of green. She also decided to make a bowl of chocolate frosting. She'd use that for the path. And eat the rest. Straight from the bowl with a spoon.

Still, given tubes as tools, the finished product would resemble nothing if not fridge art. It was a primitive art form, cake decorating. Dare she say it, a childish art form. Suitable for children. It could have no nuance, no complexity ...

She started applying the frosting with a knife. A dull butter knife she found in one of the drawers. It's how many painters applied their paint. Maybe she could get it to work ...

But even if she did, she realized, the finished product would be impermanent. By nature. It would not be preserved, studied, archived, available to future generations. It was, after all, women's work. It would disappear. It would be like it had never existed.

Worse, it would disappear not because it had been ignored or thrown away, but because it had been eaten. Consumed by others. Devoured. By others. Women prepared food. It was essential for life. And yet.

They themselves *were* food. Gestation. Lactation.

"Ladies, remember to plan ahead!" The cake decorating teacher had suddenly appeared beside Kat. She frowned at the messy path into the messier forest with which Kat had covered her cake. And then she frowned at Kat. "You haven't left any room for 'Happy Birthday, Daniel'!"

ExAcademe: I think academia must also take some of the blame, for the Gender Recognition Acts, because the whole notion of identity politics started there.

DrWho: Yes, but the notion was simply that of recognizing the influence of identity, the sociopolitical implications of one's identity. We never intended it to morph into 'I am whatever I *say* I am.' Yes, in some respects you create your own identity, with your dreams, your aspirations, your choices, your skills. But in other respects, it's created for you. By biology. The objective facts of sex, skin color, height, facial features, somatotype, etc.

GenJen: I agree. Once out of academia, identity became a political tool, and, or then, a fashion. Add gender awareness, or rather sex awareness, or rather sexual orientation ...

    ↳ **Word:** Yes, they all get conflated by minds not interested in careful distinctions!

        ↳ **ExAcademe:** Or truth! Reality!

    ↳ **Word:** And if we'd named it correctly, sex identity, maybe it wouldn't have become such a thing. Because really, how many people want to go around identifying themselves by their sex?

 ↳ **ThinkAboutIt:** Everyone. Man. Woman. Mr. Ms. Try replacing 'man' and 'woman' with 'person' and see what happens. And there isn't even an option with which to replace Mr. and Ms. unless you have a Ph.D. or an M.D.

 ↳ **Word:** Yes, but that's just habit, don't you think? If 'person' became as common, didn't seem awkward, wouldn't most people choose it?

 ↳ **ThinkAboutIt:** I don't think so. I think a lot of people *like* being identified by their sex. Especially when they're between 20 and 40, when they're feeling so very sexual.

↳ **RadFemRocks:** The whole notion of identifying yourself by your sex *or* your gender is ridiculous. It would be so much better if people used, as DrWho pointed out, their dreams, aspirations, choices, skills.

 ↳ **LovesSarcasm:** Their what?

↳ **ThinkAboutIt:** I'd put identity based on sexual orientation and even ancestry into the same category as that based on sex, skin color, and so on. Identifying yourself by *any* attributes over which you have no choice is lazy. And dangerous.

DrWho: But it's not a focus on identity per se that has caused so many problems; it's an acceptance of identity by self-proclamation. At least when the proclamation is about one's sex. Rather than, say, one's aspirations.

 ↳ **RiseUp:** Yes! 'I am a woman *if I say* I'm a woman.' 'I am a woman *because I feel* like a woman.'

ᒪ **BigRed:** Whatever the fuck that means.

ᒪ **SeeJaneScream:** Exactly. And as Meghan Murphy put it, "To create legislation around something so vague and undefinable seems odd to me, if not dangerous."

ᒪ **RadFemRocks:** Which leads to 'And I am entitled to women's rights if I say I'm a woman.'

ᒪ **LoveSarcasm:** 'Women's rights'? We have rights? Since when?

DrWho: The whole 'I feel like a woman' is nonsense. How do they know? If you aren't a dog, how do you know what it feels like to *be* a dog?

GenJen: But they claim they *are* a dog. Deep down inside.

DrWho: Well, they're wrong. They're delusional.

ᒪ **LovesSarcasm:** Deep down inside.

GenJen: I agree. The best they can do is extrapolate.

ᒪ **BigRed:** And it looks like they're extrapolating from fake women. Celebrities who are performing. Because most real women do not look or act like most transwomen. Talk about going overboard!

ᒪ **TeeTee:** But now *you're* the one who's extrapolating. From celebrities who are performing. Or are you really using your experience of *actual* transwomen you know?

  ↳ **LadyParts:** I'll tell you motherfuckers why we go overboard. We don't want to get fucking killed.

    ↳ **ExAcademe:** Fair enough. In a world fond of dichotomies, the grey area can be fatal. Better to be either male or female, man or woman.

    ↳ **BigRed:** And I'd just like to point out, LadyParts, that it's *men* who would kill you. So why don't you just fuck off and take your anger to the nearest MRA blog?

  ↳ **ANewMan:** Yeah, just shut the fuck up. It takes a lot of courage to be trans.

    ↳ **RiseUp:** Well, I think it's cowardly. I take it, ANewMan, that you're a transman. Okay. You don't want to perform femininity? So don't. Have the courage to be female and *not* do that shit. Join the rest of us who challenge the gender stereotypes. You want male privilege. I get that. You want the better jobs, the better pay. You want to be taken seriously in the workplace. I get all that. But if you become male to get all that, you're just thinking of yourself. Why not fight for *women* to get all that too? Why not fight against gender stereotypes, against sexism, against patriarchy? You're giving up. You're giving in.

    ↳ **GenJen:** I agree. You're just going to the other side of the binary.

RadFemRocks: Either way, that's all gender. Sex is biological. I feel female because my frickin' uterus hurts every month.

↳ **BigRed:** Good point. If they truly felt female, why would they *need* estrogen injections etc.?

↳ **Word:** And if they were already really women, why the prefix 'trans'?

ThinkAboutIt: But it's not so black and white, is it? I mean, is it so easy to separate the two? Gender and sex? If I don't feel particularly violent, is that due to my gender, my upbringing as a female, or due to my sex, to my low testosterone levels?

DrWho: Either way, apart from the clearly physical things, like uterus pain, how can you know what it's like to feel female until you've been male? How can you know what it's like to feel healthy until you've been sick?

↳ **SeeJaneScream:** I can tell you what it's like to feel like a woman, without having been a man. It feels like shit. To be marginalized, dismissed. To be patronized, infantilized. To be objectified, reduced.

↳ **Shazaam:** Which begs the question, even if they *do* feel like a woman, why would they want to transition? I mean, what are the advantages of passing as female? Are MtFs that clueless about sexism? Are they buying into the princess shit?

SeeJaneScream: You know what bothers me is that these men are getting their surgery, their *expensive* surgery, covered by our tax money.

↳ **Shazaam:** WTF? Really? I assumed they'd have to pay out of their own pocket because it would be considered cosmetic surgery.

    ↳ **SeeJaneScream:** Yeah, because it is just that, isn't it?

Abby8: It's insane to allow a man to insist he's a woman and then be able to apply for women's scholarships.

    ↳ **LovesScience:** Well, it's insane for there to *be* women's scholarships.

        ↳ **Dick:** Yeah, talk about discrimination based on sex! You all say you want equal treatment, but do you ever refuse all the special perks thrown your way? You women expect men to pay your way, right from the get go. Try working for a living once in a while, why dontcha?

            ↳ **SeeJaneScream:** Try fucking off once in a while, why dontcha?

    ↳ **ExAcademe:** Not in a society that not too long ago denied women entry to universities. Not in a society that pays women 60% of what it pays men.

    ↳ **LovesScience:** Okay, but what I meant was that academic ability shouldn't be sex-coded!

    ↳ **ExAcademe:** In theory, I agree. But until our practice catches up with theory ...

    ↳ **LovesScience:** But if we continue to use warped theory to determine our practice ...

GenJen: It's downright fraudulent for a man to insist he's a woman, change his driver's licence, then pay less on his automobile insurance.

↳ **LovesScience:** Well, again, there shouldn't *be* different rates for men and women.

↳ **ExAcademe:** But the accident rate is significantly different.

↳ **LovesScience:** As a whole, but *not all men* are reckless drivers. *Not all women* are safe drivers. So why don't we just consider people to be good drivers until they prove otherwise? You know, innocent until proven guilty. Once you've been charged with speeding or drinking while drunk, then your premium can go up.

Carol33: It's also insane to have sports divided by sex.

↳ **BigRed:** Not in a society in which sports overwhelmingly favour male bodies. Read upthread!

ThinkAboutIt: I agree we need to discuss these things, figure out when the discrimination is justified and when it's not, but the thing is, if you're even the least bit critical about what transpeople demand, all hell breaks loose.

↳ **LovesSarcasm:** And the problem is?

BigRed: Yes, their sense of entitlement is over the top.

RadFemRocks: Just proves they're men.

GenJen: Remember the cupcake thing?

↳ **BigRed:** God, yes! Decorating cupcakes to look like vulvas was deemed to be *oppressive* toward transwomen. It was *violence* toward transwomen. Because it *excluded* them. Give me a break!

SeeJaneScream: It just makes me want to shout, Grow the fuck up! I mean, women have been excluded, from so many things, for *centuries*, and have you seen *us* throw fucking tantrums? And talk about the pot calling the kettle black. I read a post at a trans site just the other day saying that people who don't accept that sex is determined by an individual's feelings or preferences are fascists and— wait for it—*they should be killed.*

ThinkAboutIt: I think we have to be cautious about rejecting transpeople's reactions simply because women have experienced the same thing for centuries and *not* responded that way. Or not had that response taken seriously. (Because some of us *have* gotten quite angry about it!) Maybe it should go the other way around. For example, what if we'd called *our* exclusion *oppressive* and *violence* all these centuries?

RadFemRocks: But we *have* been calling misogyny, at least, *oppressive. And* we've been calling some of it *violence.*

Word: But, and, we have to be careful. If we expand the definition of a word too far, it becomes meaningless. Exclusion isn't always oppressive. And by itself, it certainly isn't violence.

BigRed: I agree. The heart of the problem is the silly notion that inclusiveness is (always) good, exclusiveness (always) bad. That's an indefensible position. It's good/justified to exclude pedophiles from children's playgrounds. It's reasonable/justified to exclude men from studies about IUD effectiveness.

    ⌐ **LoveSarcasm:** We have to *defend* our positions now? We can't just believe whatever we want, regardless of reasonability?

RadFemRocks: I'm reminded of a post I saw on FeministCurrent about how these things—the cupcake decorations, for example, and refusing to call transmen 'women'—hurts their feelings. The response was a pointed "Why are *women's* feelings being ignored in all of this?" Transpeople must be allowed to use women's restrooms, must be allowed to work at women's shelters, because to exclude them is offensive, blah blah. What about the offense to the women who use those restrooms, to the women who access those shelters?

GenJen: On that note, I'd like to quote from Sharon Thrace's "Destruction of a Marriage: My Husband's Descent into Transgenderism"(in *Female Erasure*, ed. Ruth Barrett, p.454):

"[Gender identity] holds that 'feeling like a woman' (whatever that means) is the same as *being* a woman. It's a callous disregard for our lifetime of oppression, the limits placed upon our participation in society, the ever-present threat of rape we face. It's an erasure of the quarter of our lives we spend managing bleeding and pain, the constant diligence we must employ to prevent pregnancy. It's a gross insensitivity of the staggering percentage of us who are victims of sexual assault, starting in childhood. We face these realities because we have female bodies and because of how men treat people who inhabit such bodies. There exists no fashion choice nor inner angst that can bring men closer to this experience. ... Kris likes to complain that I don't recognize him as a woman, something he sees as a great offense. But the irony is that he does not recognize *me* as a woman. ... My biology is not irrelevant. My experience cannot be duplicated by trying on my clothes."

She goes on to say this brilliant bit:

"It takes a great deal of male privilege to 'choose' your gender, as if gender weren't a set of obligations and proscriptions designed to keep women physically, emotionally, and financially handicapped."

So have you had a chance to read the pamphlets I gave you?" Dr. Gagnon looked at her from across her desk.

"Yes."

"And?"

"The APA is so fucked up." She continued before he had a chance to object to her language. "*Why Are Some People Transgender?* the pamphlet asks. Their answer?" She pulled the pamphlet out of her pocket—with mixed feelings, she'd started wearing an apron because it *had* pockets—and read. "*Many experts believe that biological factors such as genetic influences and prenatal hormone levels, early experiences, and experiences later in adolescence or adulthood may all contribute to the development of transgender identities.*

"Um, no. People are transgender because they are intelligent and thoughtful enough to realize that gendered behaviours are typically constraining and, in the case of women, that feminine behaviours in particular are subordinating. And so, they reject them; they refuse to conform to the gender expectations aligned to their sex. Or because they simply want to be: they *like* loose clothing and philosophy.

She pressed on. "*How Does Someone Know They Are Transgender?* the pamphlet then asks. Their answer? *They may have vague feelings of 'not fitting in' with people of their assigned sex or specific wishes to be something other than their assigned sex. Others become aware of their transgender identities or begin to explore and experience gender-nonconforming attitudes and behaviors during adolescence or much later in life.*

"First, I doubt I was *assigned* a sex. Most likely, the delivering obstetrician correctly *identified* my sex, based on external genitalia. I get that in the case of intersexed people," she qualified, "sex is 'assigned' and maybe the obstetrician made a mistake or maybe the evidence on which he or she based his or her decision wasn't the strongest, most influential, bit, because there was a mismatch of chromosomes, ovaries or testicles, hormones, and/or vagina or penis, but that happens in less than 0.1%. One in 1500.

"And second," she returned to the main point, "I know I'm a writer because when I write, I actually realize that that's what I'm doing. Similarly, when I refuse to wear make-up and high heels, I know I'm doing it. I'm that aware." She gave him a moment. "And I know it's transgressive. I'm also that aware." Another moment. "I *know* what the gender expectations are in our society, so I know when I'm refusing to meet them. *That's* how I know I'm transgender."

He opened his mouth, but she put up her hand to stop him. From interrupting. From talking.

"One doesn't *become aware* of one's gender identity. One *creates* it. One *chooses* it. Unlike one's sex, sexual orientation, height, skin colour, eye colour ... *gender is not a biological given.* It's an arbitrary collection of preferences that 'society' says should you should adopt: the so-called feminine collection is supposed to be adopted by female people, and the so-called masculine collection is supposed to be adopted by male people."

"But—"

"As for the DSM," she pulled that print-out from her pocket and started reading, "the definition of *Gender Dysphoria* is *A marked incongruence between one's experienced/expressed gender and assigned gender, of at least 6 months' duration—* Well, hell yes," she looked up, "I've been experiencing a *marked incongruence* since childhood. Whenever I experience or express aggression, strength, initiative, a fondness for motorcycles, an aversion to pastels …"

She resumed reading. "*—as manifested by at least two of the following. One. A marked incongruence between one's gender and primary and/or secondary sex characteristics.* That's oddly put. It *presumes* some sort of *congruence* between gender and primary and/or secondary sex characteristics. How is the forementioned aggression, strength, initiative, fondness for motorcycles, or aversion to pastels connected to, for example, having ovaries? Or an enlarged larynx? Could you please explain that?"

He could not.

"*Two. A strong desire to be rid of one's primary and/or secondary sex characteristics because of a marked incongruence with one's experienced/expressed gender.* No. This one doesn't apply to me. Because of the *because.*"

She gave him a moment to process that.

"*Three. A strong desire for the primary and/or secondary sex characteristics of the other gender.* No again. I have a *mild* desire for *some* of the very peripheral male characteristics."

"But you admit you don't like your body. Your female body."

She nodded. "I admit I don't like my female body. I've never liked having breasts. The pleasure they might give during sexual interaction was nothing compared to the displeasure they caused when I ran. Bags of fat flopping on my chest— And since I did the latter far more frequently than the former…

"Plus, breasts are a can't-miss-it announcement that I'm female."

"And you don't want to be female?" Aha! He had her!

"Would *you* want to be subordinated every day in almost every way? Would you like a 40% pay cut, for starters?"

He didn't respond.

"And yes, I have had a strong desire to be rid of my uterus—who *likes* menstruating once a month? The pain. The messiness. The inconvenience. And since I never intended to become a mother, what was the point? Five days a month of pain for thirty years for nothing! An evolutionary mistake if there ever was one."

"But it's natural!"

"Natural doesn't mean smart. Evolution doesn't mean intelligent design. *Intelligent design* doesn't even mean intelligent design."

That stopped him. For a few moments.

"So why *didn't* you get a hysterectomy?"

"Honestly? It didn't occur to me. Or maybe it did and I thought, I had been led to believe, that there were serious negative health consequences. Unlike for a mastectomy and a tubal cauterization."

"So you'd rather be a man."

"What? No. I wouldn't like having a male body either. Having all that 'junk' dangling down between my legs? That'd be worse than having breasts. And facial hair? I hate beards and mustaches, so while I don't mind hair on my legs and so don't shave, I *would* shave my face. And even though that's a lot less time-consuming than shaving one's legs, because there's less surface area, it'd be a hassle. I'd probably have to do it every day. My father had to. Twice, if he was going out in the evening. And an Adam's apple? No thanks. Don't like the lines. A higher center of gravity? Probably not. And seven times as much testosterone coursing through my body? *Definitely* not.

"I would like to be able to develop muscle a bit more easily," she conceded. "And I would like less subcutaneous fat. But that's about it."

"So," he was struggling to keep up, "if you don't like having a female body and you wouldn't like having a male body ..."

"Yes? You need to finish your sentence."

"Well, what else *is* there?"

So lacking in imagination.

"A neutered body. An asexual body. That'd be nice. An lean, strong, flexible, coordinated, asexual body. That's what I'd like."

She turned her attention back to the APA print-out.

"*Four. A strong desire to be of the other gender or some alternative gender different from one's assigned gender.*" She looked up. "No. I don't want to be some *other* gender. I don't want *any* arbitrary, let alone crippling, package of attributes assigned to me, expected of me, because of my sex."

"So—you deny that you've been crossdressing?"

"What?" Oh. She made the connection. Dress is gendered. And her clothing has been male. At least partly. "I've never thought of it that way. As I thought I explained in our last session, I wear what I wear not according to whether it's sold in the women's department or the men's department, but according to what I *want* to wear. And I look in both departments for what I want—for what fits, for what feels comfortable, for the colour I like, for the style I like—and then I buy it. Sometimes I happen to find it in the women's department, sometimes I happen to find it in the men's department, and sometimes I don't find it anywhere."

"And your hair?"

"What about my hair?"

"It's short."

"Astute observation."

He missed that in his eagerness to explain to her—
"Women typically have long hair. The few that have short hair
have it styled. Yours looks like you just wash-and-go."

"Which is what men do?"

He nodded.

"Well, again, I don't have short hair because that's male; I
have short hair because short hair doesn't get in my eyes and it's
easy to brush. In fact, it doesn't even *need* to be brushed. It's
easier than long hair to wash-and-go, and I wash-and-go," she
anticipated, "not because that's the male way, but because I don't
want to spend time styling it." After she showered, she ran her
fingers through her hair a few times front to back, and that was
that. Good to go.

"And you don't shave your legs. Et cetera."

"Again, not because I want to be a man, but because I've got
better things to do with my time and energy." Why was he being
so dense?

She turned back to the print-out.

"*Five. A strong desire to be treated as the other gender or some
alternative gender different from one's assigned gender.* Yes.
Definitely yes on this point. Assuming the alignment between
masculinity and male. I'd like to be taken seriously. I'd like to be
given the jobs, the promotions, the salaries, I deserve. For
starters. I hate that I can't escape from being second-class, as
Gwyneth Jones put it. I'd like to be the norm, not the exception
in the margin, the special case subject to compartmentalization."

"So you *do* want to change your sex."

"No." She sighed. "I want to be treated *like* a man. In some
respects. Men get taken seriously. For example. Men are rewarded,
more often than women, according to merit. For example."

He wasn't listening to her. Case in point. "Men are *listened
to.*" She stared at him. He just stared back.

"And even if I *did* want to be male rather than female, even if I *did* want to be a man rather than a woman, is that really so surprising? Can you really not understand why girls *don't* want to grow up to be women? Almost half of them, when they're between sixteen and eighteen, experience unwanted sexual touching. Never mind the near non-existent rights to their own reproductive bodies. Every single one of them has been called a slut or a cunt or a cow or a bitch. Most are called that at least once a day. Every single one of them is on a diet."

She turned back again to the print-out.

"*Six. A strong conviction that one has the typical feelings and reactions of the other gender or some alternative gender different from one's assigned gender.* Yes. I feel angry. A lot. For starters. Though why anger is associated with masculinity, I have no idea.

"Lastly," she concluded, "the DSM says the condition must be associated with *clinically significant distress or impairment in social, occupational, or other important areas of functioning.* I don't know that I experience *clinically significant distress*, but I suspect that being a non-feminine female in our society is an impairment. In social and occupational areas."

"So you agree with the diagnosis?" he asked, triumphantly. "You've confirmed manifestation of two of the elements."

"Yes. In fact, I'd argue that *all* mentally *healthy* people, *all sane* people, have gender dysphoria. They reject, quite reasonably, the gender straitjacket forced on them by our society. Specifically, many women experience gender dysphoria because we do not identify as idiots and fuck toys and that is what gender dictates we be."

He studied her for a long moment. He even steepled his fingers. Making sure she knew that he was *thinking*.

"We'll start with talk therapy and then move on to reparative therapy, how does that sound?"

How does that sound? It sounds like you think you're talking to a child.

"So you're just going to ignore my implied objection?" You're not going to take me seriously. "To the classification of gender dysphoria as a mental illness? You don't think you have to, I don't know, *justify* its status *as* a mental illness?"

"Forty-five percent of sixteen to twenty-five year-olds who feel drawn to the gender that does not match their sex attempt suicide. Isn't that justification enough?"

"No," she surprised him. "A decision to commit suicide may be rational. Even healthy. But more to the point, here and now, how do you determine that the mentioned incongruence is evidence of gender dysphoria rather than evidence of gender rejection? Why don't you consider gender dysphoria to *justify* gender *rejection?*"

"Forty-five percent! Those of us in the psychiatric profession are merely trying to help."

"Well," she sighed, "you're going about it the wrong way. You want to help? Subvert gender. It's *gender* that's mentally ill."

No response.

"It seems to me," she ventured, "that the problem isn't so much with those of us who are female but feel strong, for example, or those of us who are male but feel sensitive, but with those of you who insist that females be weak and males be insensitive, those of you who *construct* gender, *assigning* it to people on the basis of their sex."

Still no response.

She sighed again. "What does reparative therapy include?"

"It can involve any one or more of a number of techniques," he replied enthusiastically, "such as reinforcement, aversion, and so on. I don't want to get too technical here." Because you surely wouldn't understand. "The basis is that some damage has been done and it needs repair. For example, a woman's desire to become a man is often a rational and unconscious attempt to self-repair feelings of inferiority."

Well, duh.

"And then there are a number of faith-based therapies, if you're so inclined."

"I am not. So inclined."

He nodded. "And finally, there are a number of medical therapies available. For example, sometimes a woman's desire to become a man is the result of an estrogen deficiency."

She thought about that. Certainly estrogen affected other desires; any self-aware woman noticed that. But who determined what was 'deficiency'? "You can measure my estrogen levels?"

He nodded again. "And progesterone and testosterone."

Then again, what would be the point? She was fine with the way she was. And the way she had been. For surely, her hormone levels had changed throughout the course of her life. It was society that had a problem with it.

Despite being roommates, and having a lot in common—well, having *had* a lot in common—Kat and Holly didn't see much of each other. Holly was usually gone before Kat got up, or so focussed on 'getting ready' that she ignored her. Some days, Kat got the feeling that she didn't really *want* to associate with her. At least, she didn't want to be *seen* associating with her. Perhaps because Kat wasn't co-operating. Kat sighed. Was a time Holly wouldn't've cooperated either. Had the whole firefighter thing and then the search-and-rescue thing broken her?

Near the end of her second week at the institution, a young woman—well, in her forties, to Kat's sixties—approached Kat as she was outside walking about, around and around, head down, trying to be … alone.

"Professor Jones?" the woman asked tentatively.

Kat paused and looked up, startled at the title. "Yes?"

The woman waited. Apparently for recognition.

"I'm sorry, I—"

"Liz? From your Social Ethics class? You don't remember?" She seemed crestfallen.

"Liz? Of course!"

The woman reached out her hand, changed her mind, then gave Kat a quick hug. Kat automatically stiffened. Tried not to. Failed.

"Yeah, I'm not a hugger either. But."

Women were supposed to hug each other. Well, actually, they were supposed to hug everyone. Apparently.

"Yeah."

Kat resumed walking, gesturing to Liz to walk with her.

"I didn't recognize you without your buzzcut and your Doc Martens!"

Liz was wearing a blouse, a skirt, and heels. And looking very uncomfortable about it.

"But yes, I do remember you! You're the only student ever to make a pass at me!"

"In my defence," Liz blushed as she tried to keep up in the damn heels, "I'm probably not the only student ever to mis-take you for a lesbian though."

Kat turned to her, surprised. "Really?"

She thought about that as they continued walking. Slowly.

"That would explain at least some of the hostility," she realized. Out loud. "At least from the male students."

She stopped then and stuck a foot out from under her long dress. "You should check the boutique for a pair of nurse's shoes."

"I did," Nancy replied. "I do. Size sixes go fast."

"Ah." They resumed walking. Slowly. "I thought all the anger, and resentment, and whatever, was just, you know, immaturity. Men not being able to handle a woman in a position of authority over them."

"Oh it was definitely that, but— You remember Clark?"

Kat nodded. "Clark was the one who got me fired. Well, not rehired. Sessionals don't actually get fired."

"Really? I didn't know that. Not about sessionals not getting fired, but about Clark being— We all knew he started a petition, claiming that you didn't respect the students, that you made fun of them, and a whole bunch of other shit, but— The Dean believed it?" She turned to her, aghast.

"The customer is always right," Kat said wryly.

"Wow. Didn't know students could have so much power. Otherwise, maybe we ... I should have ..."

"The *male* customer is always right," Kat amended.

Liz didn't respond. She was concentrating on walking. A blister was forming on her right foot.

"But you're saying that a lot of students thought I was lesbian?" Kat circled back.

"Well, yeah."

"Why?" She truly wanted to know.

"The way you dressed, the way you walked, the way you carried yourself. No make-up. No boyfriend. No husband. No kids." The list came so easily.

"Not every straight woman performs femininity," Kat protested.

"No, but most do, don't they?"

Kat considered that. "I suppose. Maybe more in your generation than in mine. But yeah, maybe most of the straight women who aren't particularly feminine, that I've seen, are actually lesbian."

"That's why Andrea—remember the fuss she made when you showed up wearing some guy's pajama top?"

"It wasn't 'some guy's pajama top'! It was something I'd bought it at the Goodwill! It was burgundy, which I like. It was cotton, which I like. And it was very loose-fitting, which I also like."

"So it didn't occur to you that some students might have thought that you wore it to brag about what you'd done the night before?"

"What?" Kat was so dumbfounded she stopped walking.

"That's what Andrea thought. She thought you were broadcasting a one-nighter."

Kat's jaw dropped. "Why the hell would I broadcast that?"

"And since she'd thought you were a lesbian, the fact that it was a *men's* pajama top ..."

Kat was silent. Working hard to rewrite her memories of that class, that day, that week, that term ...

"God, I'm so clueless," she finally said. Summing up. Everything.

"Well, I wouldn't say you're *that* clueless ..." Liz grinned.

"That's what comes of not having any friends," Kat said when they resumed walking. "Of not—"

"Fuck this," Liz muttered, bending down and taking off her shoes. "Women take off their heels sometimes, don't they?" She looked around furtively. Where was the nearest camera?

"Yes," Kat said, then continued dryly, "when they're walking on a sandy beach in the moonlight with a tall, dark, and handsome stranger. A tall, dark, and handsome *male* stranger."

Liz discovered that walking shoeless on the sidewalk was almost as bad. Kat nudged her onto the grass and moved to walk alongside, at the edge of the sidewalk, hopefully blocking her some of the time. For surely it was inappropriate for women to walk barefoot on the grass. Unless they had flowers in their hair. And were hand-in-hand with a tall, dark, and handsome male stranger.

"That's what comes," she continued her other line of thought, "of not being subject to any sort of peer pressure or influence or reaction. One's opinions and actions become completely independent, completely ... *true*. None of that—what you said about my wearing that top—not of that even occurred to me. I liked the colour, the fabric, and the fit. End of story. For me."

Liz nodded.

"If so many of my students thought I was a lesbian," Kat continued to work through the rewrite, "I wonder how many other people have thought I was a lesbian. That could explain a lot of, well, not only a lot of what happened at Nipissing, but a lot of what's happened throughout my life."

"Like why you haven't seen a lot of men's pajama tops," Liz grinned.

Kat smiled, then nodded.

"I'd always thought it was because I was smart. Men don't like women who are smart. Smarter than them. Which is, usually, just smart." She grimaced.

"I think people in general resent intelligence," Liz suggested. "Now."

Kat thought about that. "You may be right. That's very insightful."

Liz blushed. Again.

"Men don't like women who are more competent than them either," Liz said. "And I imagine you're pretty competent. You're a runner, right? And you play the piano?"

"Used to be. And used to be." She turned to her. "How did you know that?"

"I saw you sometimes. On your lunch break or between classes or whatever. You used to go for a run in the woods by the campus."

"Oh yeah." She'd forgotten that. It had happened during only one term, when she'd had an awkward schedule. Not enough time to go into town between classes, but too much time to just sit in the library or the cafeteria—sessionals didn't have an office.

"And I was shy. I thought that was another reason. For my not having any friends."

"Probably. I'm shy too. And without the local lesbian community, I would have been just as friendless. Men hate us. Because we're not available to them. Sexually. And in so many other ways. We're not their cheerleaders. But women hate us too."

"Why? You'd think they'd like that you're not competition."

"I think they see us as a challenge to their conformity. To femininity. We—well, butch lesbians, at least—rub their faces in the fact that women don't *have* to wear make-up and heels. Well, *didn't* have to."

They were silent for a moment.

"I thought women hated me because I rubbed their faces in the fact that women don't have to have a husband and kids."

"Probably that too."

"Pity there's no community for straight women who look butch. Straight women who remain unmarried. Child-free."

Liz nodded.

Because, Kat wondered, not for the first time, where *were* all the heterosexual women who looked like butch dykes? Who just … didn't want to wear make-up and fussy clothes and jewelry, the heterosexual women who wanted to run and ride motorcycles … None of that was necessarily associated with sexual orientation. How could it be? That alignment was as much bullshit as the alignment with sex. As lipstick lesbians demonstrated.

"If you'd lived in Toronto," Liz said, "at least you could have joined the local Mensa group or something. Found some friends there maybe."

Kat nodded. But she wasn't a group person. Then again, maybe it was just that she'd never found the right group.

"So how is it you're here?" Kat changed the topic. "If it isn't impolite to ask. I mean, you're clearly not mentally ill."

"Oh but clearly I am. All lesbians actually want to be men, don't you know?"

"Don't tell me you've been charged with Gender Fraud too."

"Is that why *you're* here?"

Kat nodded.

"I was *arrested* for Gender Fraud," Liz said, "but now that I'm here, I'm being treated for homosexuality."

"That's a mental illness? Again?"

Liz nodded.

"Jeezus. What the fuck *happened?* When I wasn't looking," she added.

Liz didn't reply.

"We have *got* to get out of here. Doesn't anyone know how behind North Bay is?"

"Actually, it's so behind, it's at the front. This whole gender fraud dragnet started in Toronto. We were organized enough to see it coming. Lesbians fled the city in droves, heading for small towns that were off grid, so to speak."

"Off grid?"

"Social media being 'grid'."

"Ah. But North Bay has internet access!"

"Yes, but social media engagement here doesn't even come close to what it is in bigger cities. Paradoxically."

Kat thought about that. It *was* a paradox.

"I take it you don't have a Facebook page," Liz said.

Kat shook her head.

"Or a Twitter account."

She shook her head again.

"You probably don't even know what a hashtag is."

"I know it used to be called a 'sharp' or a 'number' sign. Why they had to give it yet another name …"

"Because it now has another meaning."

Kat hesitated, then nodded in partial concession.

"Social media is subject to such a high level of social contagion, it's scarey."

"You're saying all this is happening because of social media?"

"If you look back, over just the last ten years, which is when social media really took off, what happened to feminism? It got hijacked, became a bad thing. And the whole trans thing? Never would've become so … infectious. So infectious that governments were carried along, to the point of making legislative changes that were ridiculous. You're a woman if you say you're a woman, if you *feel* like a woman," Liz snorted.

Kat saw the merit of her analysis.

"So all this gender fraud frenzy—"

"Is a case in point. So," Liz returned to her earlier point, "suddenly it was all the rural places that were safe. For lesbians."

"And gender outlaws such as myself. Which is why I wasn't arrested until now."

Liz nodded.

They walked another lap.

"So you finished your degree, I take it?"

"I did. And then some. I've actually got a Master's in History now."

"Good for you! Did you get any grants for your grad school studies?" She remembered seeing Liz working at the Dairy Queen to pay for her tuition and her books …

She shook her hand. "There weren't any that I knew about that I could apply for."

"You should have applied for one of the grants they give to Native students."

"But—"

"You could've just told them that you were. A Native Canadian. That you *felt* like a Native Canadian."

Liz grinned.

"You like nature, right? You go hiking through the forest? You paddle a canoe?"

"That is such a stereotype."

"Yeah, well, when's the last time you saw a transwoman?"

"Good point. Though it's interesting that they go for the slutty look rather than the matronly look."

"Yeah …" Kat thought about that for a few moments, then circled back. "Get yourself a pair of moccasins," Kat said. "Maybe you can get your Ph.D."

At that, Liz burst out laughing.

"Please tell me you were able to do something with that Master's degree," Kat said a short while later. "I mean, you're not still working at the Dairy Queen, are you?"

"Well," she grinned, "I was a sessional at Nipissing for a while—"

"No!"

"Yes!"

"New Dean. And their History Department is a little better, a little bigger, than their Philosophy Department."

"Still."

"Still," she agreed.

"What was your thesis on?"

Again, Liz grinned. "The History of Social Media."

"Seriously? I'd like to read it! I *should* read it! Is that possible? I mean, here? Hang on," Kat backed up, "you said 'for a while'—so … now?"

"Now I'm a freelance social media manager. A lot of people are like you. Like I think you are. They need to be on social media. You're a published author. You should definitely be on social media! Establish a fan base. Well, *expand* your fan base—"

"Right the first time."

"Okay, but, either way, you really should be on social media. And I'll bet you really don't want to be."

"I really don't want to be," Kat agreed.

"So you hire someone like me and I act as sort of your ghostwriter."

"Really?"

"Really."

"Isn't that a bit dishonest?"

"It is. It can be," she corrected. "But I put a disclaimer at the top of all the accounts I manage. Saying 'This account is managed by …' and I use whatever handle I'm using."

"Yeah, but 'managed by' isn't the same as 'written by'."

"It is now. At least, it's understood to be the same."

"Not by me."

"No, not by people like you."

"People like me?" She hadn't missed the earlier reference.

"People of the pre-social media generation. You need to read my thesis," Liz added, smiling.

"Yeah. I guess it's like 'going on a date' now means 'going to have sex'."

"Well I don't think it's quite the same. I think *men* think that's what it means. But a lot of women think otherwise. That's partly what led to the whole #metoo phenomenon. It's not as simple as saying that men rape more often now. Though I'm sure they do. They watch porn more often now. And porn is more often violent. But I think, additionally, a fundamental disjunct has formed between men's understanding and women's understanding of things."

"Hang on," again Kat backed up, "how did you know I was a published author?"

"I've been following you. Not stalking you," she hastened to qualify. "I'm over my crush. Mostly."

Kat grinned. As did Liz.

"But you're an interesting person. And every now and then I've been curious as to what you've been up to. A simple google search … I've read your novels, by the way. They're brilliant. You really do need to be on social media. The entire feminist community should know about your work!"

"Okay, once we're both out …"

They walked in silence for a bit.

"So how are they 'treating' your homosexuality?"

"For now, talk therapy. I suspect aversive conditioning is a distinct possibility. Hopefully, corrective rape is not."

"You're— You're serious." Kat was horrified. "Jeezus. But— They wouldn't, would they?"

"I don't know. It's a thing now. On the outside. Men raping lesbians. The straight community wants us to be straight, and the trans community wants us to transition," she sighed. "Just being lesbian isn't legitimate anymore."

"But I thought the trans movement was about sex and gender. Not sexual orientation," Kat was confused.

"Sexual orientation is part of gender now, I guess. If you want to be attracted to women, you'd better be male."

"So wouldn't they just want you to transition? Here? Wouldn't that be your … treatment? I can't believe I said 'just'," she added.

"Maybe. If I don't become straight. And feminine. That's the current objective. For getting out."

S o, Katherine, you've been with us for a couple weeks," said Mary-Anne, looking like a princess to Kat's cinderwench, as she opened their weekly chat the following morning. Their mandatory weekly chat. "How would you say it's going?"

"It's not going well?" Kat stifled a laugh. A maniacal laugh.

"I would agree. Looking at your demerit reports for the last two weeks, I have to say that you're well on your way to extending your stay with us. Beyond the six months."

Kat looked up, startled.

"Is that what you want?"

Yeah, that's definitely what she wanted. God, she hated Mary-Anne's tone. Did it take practice or did it just come naturally? She'd always wondered. Because so many people talked to her like that. So many people treated her like she was a child. Had done so all her life. She'd thought that once she hit forty … But no. Was it because she wasn't married? Wasn't a parent? Spouse and kids seemed to be the gold standards of adulthood. Go figure. She figured maintaining your autonomy and using contraception would be indicators of maturity.

"Katherine? Is that what you want?"

"No, of course not. I'm so sorry. How can I rectify the situation?"

"Well, as you know, five gold stars erase one demerit point, but apart from that—"

"Gold stars?" She stifled another laugh.

"Yes. Didn't you read your orientation package?"

Actually, she had finally gotten around to reading it, but ... She hadn't been processing on all cylinders in the early days. Still wasn't.

Mary-Anne opened one of her desk drawers and took out a sheet of paper. She stood up, walked a few steps to a photocopier, made a copy, then handed it to Kat. It looked vaguely familiar. The double-columned list. Decorated with sad faces and gold stars. She must have thrown it away. Because, really, it was so implausible ... And because how the hell was she going to obtain even *one* gold star? Given her performance in the Cake Decorating class, and the Interior Design class she'd attended the day after, it was unlikely that any of her completed projects would win best-in-class.

Maybe she could make a case for a clean slate based on belated good behaviour. She decided then and there to start attending all of her assigned classes and groups. She'd make sure not to wear the same outfit twice in a row. She'd wear a bra, with the fake boobs tucked inside. She'd put on a bit of make-up. Every day. Every fucking day.

So, after just two weeks, she gave in. To get out. Hopefully, in three months. Because there was no way she could do six months. And still be herself. And if she couldn't be herself—

"Keep in mind that we're trying to give you the skills to live as a woman in the real world," Laura reprimanded that afternoon as Kat sent her knitting needles flying across the room. Pity there wasn't a dart board on the other side.

"Why does living as a woman need special skills?" she'd responded. "Other than those needed for living as a human?"

Because, she could answer her own question, she had to live in a sex-differentiated society. A society that coded *everything* by sex. The day she saw pink hammers in the hardware store—though, truth be told, there could be as good an argument for those as for pink firefighting equipment. They need not colour-code them, though. In fact, they need not even *sex*-code them. Coding by size and weight, or what have you, would be sufficient. Better, actually, because it wouldn't stigmatize larger-than-normal women and smaller-than-normal men.

"And why does it need to be learned?" Kat continued. "If it's natural … and isn't that the basis of your philosophy? That it's unnatural for me to act 'as a man'? Isn't that why it's fraudulent?"

Well, no, it was fraudulent because it denied someone else, men, of something else, their entitlements. Their socially constructed entitlements. Their *unnatural* entitlements.

She'd intended to go to the Feminine Fitness class the following morning; Holly had mentioned it the night before. Maybe she could get brownie points for attending a class that wasn't on her list. But when morning came, she decided she'd rather stay in bed.

Just as well, since, she found out later, the class was all about flat tummies and Kegels.

Be sexual, but hide the consequences. From us.

Next day, she attended her first group therapy session. The one for Anger Management. Ten women, including Kat, were seated in a circle. Kat looked around her. Every woman but one was seething with anger at having to be there. She burst out laughing.

"I'd like to start today by introducing our newest member,

Katherine," the but one spoke up. "Katherine, would you like to share with the group what you find so funny?"

"The fact that every one of us is angry about being in an Anger Management therapy group."

Several of the women smiled.

The but one woman made a note.

Oh dear.

"And you find that amusing?"

"Yes. And appropriate. Healthy. Dare I say *sane*."

"Hear, hear," one of the women said in a gruff voice.

Kat turned sharply. She recognized that voice. Sort of. The woman was large. Sloppy, some would say. Rolls of fat pushed at the shapeless beige polyester dress she wore, and her legs were thick in beige stockings. She wore maroon slippers like her dad used to wear. She had fair hair, and freckles, but … was that a bit of stubble? The badly-applied make-up didn't cover it … She suddenly placed the voice. Dell? From River Oaks?

The woman had been looking intently at her as well. When she saw Kat's flicker of recognition, she smiled briefly, then shook her head ever so slightly.

"I see. Why don't you tell the group why you're here?" the but one woman said.

"I'm here because some people can't tell the difference between justified anger and unjustified anger. And/or because they believe that even justified anger should not be felt, or at least not expressed, by women. Which makes sense if you believe, in the first case, that women are idiots, or, in the second case, that they should be complete doormats."

"What do you mean?"

"What do I mean?" She hated when people said that. It was laziness. Sheer laziness. "I mean what I said. Which words didn't you understand?"

She saw Dell smile. At the floor.

"Perhaps you can describe what made you so angry."

"The esthetician and the beautician did things to my body without my consent."

"Could you elaborate?" Another lazy response, but okay, sure.

"Elena ripped the hair off my legs, my armpits, my pubic area, and my anal area. And Lalene put some shit around my eyes and she dyed my hair. Without my consent." Kat repeated. Because *that's* what they needed to discuss. It enabled the distinction. Between justified anger and unjustified anger.

"And all that made you angry."

"You asked me to describe what made me angry. I described several things. Therefore, yes, all that made me angry."

Dell smiled again. At the floor.

"It sounds like you're getting a little angry right now."

"I am. Would you like me to describe what's making me angry?"

"Perhaps a better course of action would be for you to explain how you'll manage your anger."

"Hm." Kat considered that. "Isn't it better yet, at least in some cases, to practice anger avoidance rather than anger management?"

"Yes!" The but one woman was delighted. She was such a good Anger Management therapist!

Kat got up and left.

Kat hung out in her room until eleven, at which time she headed outside for the hour. And there she was. Sitting on one of the park benches that lined the path.

"Dell?"

"In the flesh," she grinned. "More or less," she added, vaguely gesturing at her body.

Up close, Dell looked grotesque. As grotesque as Kat felt in her peach-coloured dress, yellow knee socks, and white nursing shoes.

Kat paused, then glanced around. Where were the cameras? Just in case, she bent down and tried to give Dell a hug. It was awkward, stupid, and—stupid.

"Just sit," Dell grinned.

Kat sat.

"And keep your legs together."

"What? Oh. Right."

"And it's Delilah."

"Since— Oh. Right. Hi. I'm Katherine." It felt so odd. She'd never referred to herself as Katherine. She'd gone directly from Katie as a kid to Kat in high school. And calling Dell 'Delilah' was just so … wrong.

"A new member of the group indeed," Dell laughed. Kat had loved her laugh. It was so full, so unpretentious. "So what are *you* doing here?"

Kat told her.

"And *you?*" But as soon as she asked the question, she knew. She'd noticed the stubble. Though even without— "When did you transition? *Why* did you transition?"

"About five years ago. Because I wasn't comfortable being female."

"Who is?" But again, as soon as she'd said it— A lot of women *were* comfortable being female. Those leading unexamined lives …

"So when did *you* transition?"

"What? I didn't."

"Oh. Sorry. Thought you had top surgery. It kinda looks like … your falsies have shifted."

Kat let out a growl of annoyance, then shifted them back into place. More or less. "I *did* have top surgery. Well, a bilateral mastectomy. Stage zero. So I decided to be proactive …"

"Oh. Sorry."

"I'm not. Never liked my breasts anyway. Globs of fat on my chest? Who'd want that? And, as you may recall, I was a runner. Globs of fat *jiggling* on my chest?"

"Tell me about it."

Right. Dell's gobs of fat were significantly larger than Kat's had been.

"You are aware that's illegal now," Dell commented.

Kat's eyes widened. She hadn't been aware. But— "No, it was because—*cancer*."

"Doesn't matter."

"You're kidding." But abortions had been illegal even when the woman's life was at risk … Perhaps were again, she realized.

"What's next, illegalizing tattoos and pierced ears?"

Dell nodded. "The first if you're a woman, the second if you're a man."

"Unfuckingbelievable." Was there no end to the arbitrariness of the gender binary?

"Your cluelessness? Yeah."

Kat grinned. An easy silence followed.

"So what do you do now? *Did* you do? Now. Before." Kat wondered then, with horror, whether *any* of them would have their jobs when they got out. She was freelance, so she could resume working once she was out, hopefully, even if she couldn't keep it up while here—she had yet to look into that. But others— Did they assume every woman was a homemaker-housewife? Or working just for pin money?

"I'm the Director of Bayside."

"Bayside? The private seniors place?"

Dell nodded. They'd met at River Oaks. A government-funded seniors' residence. When Kat bought her cabin, she'd expected to support herself as a supply teacher, being within driving distance of seven high schools. But when the regular stream of supply teaching days that she'd anticipated hadn't materialized, she looked around for some sort of part-time position and landed a relief position at River Oaks. Often she just worked a night shift, doing security checks, making sure everyone was okay, but sometimes they called her in to assist with special and sometimes off-site recreation events. Between the two jobs, she usually made enough to pay the mortgage at least.

That was before she lucked out and became a sessional at Nipissing, which led to more luck, as she was then able to see the ad in *The Chronicle for Higher Education* placed by ETS looking for item writers for the GRE. That's when life became really sweet. From that point on, she could work without ever having to leave her lovely cabin in a forest on a lake. And without ever again having to deal with asshole supervisors. Or Deans. Or students. No pension or benefits, but what else was new?

"Yeah. It's not exactly like River Oaks, but it's close enough."

"And did you get that position before or after you transitioned."

"After."

"But wouldn't your references— You listed your years at River Oaks on your resume, right?"

"Yeah. But I was *Dell* with ten years' experience, not Delilah. And I used my mother's maiden surname. On all my new ID."

"Still."

"Yeah. It was a risk," Dell agreed. "But oddly enough, I don't think they made any inquiries."

"Right." It's enough to be male. "Your competence was assumed."

Dell nodded. "Ten years' experience as an Assistant Recreation Manager, a general B.A. in Psychology, an unfinished Master's in Gerontology, and a couple courses in Office Management. I was their first choice for Assistant Director. And then when the Director resigned, I was simply next in line. That's how it works. When you're a guy."

"You wouldn't've gotten anywhere near something like that at River Oaks. Even if you'd had a fucking Ph.D. in Gerontology and an MBA. You would have been a low-status and poorly-paid rec manager, *assistant* rec manager," she corrected, "for the rest of your life."

Again, Dell nodded.

"And I'll bet your size—"

"Is an asset."

Kat nodded. Men carried their extra pounds, muscle *or* fat, with pride, with confidence. Unless they were terribly obese and jiggly—and they could hide that with a stiff suit—it gave them power. It came across, on some base level, as intimidation.

"So transition was … a career move?"

"God, no. That was just a nice perk. I've never really felt like a woman."

"Well, neither have I. But that just means you reject all the gender shit and rebel against all the sexism. It doesn't mean you become a man."

"Well, I'm not, really."

"You're not taking testosterone?"

"Not anymore, but yeah, I did take testosterone. And I did get top surgery. A mastectomy. But that's it. I'm not getting a dick. I just use a bit of padding and a funnel."

"It's that important to pee while standing up? Men's restrooms have stalls. Why don't you just use those?"

Dell didn't answer. Instead, she circled back.

"If women had as much authority, as much freedom, as much personhood, as much *humanity*, as men, I wouldn't've wanted to become a man." Clearly, she'd done a lot of thinking about the matter. "Half the time though, people already thought I was a man," she added.

Kat wasn't surprised. Dell couldn't've come off as feminine even if she'd tried. She was large. Huge, even. She wore comfortable clothes, most often men's clothes, because they simply didn't make women's clothing that large. She didn't wear make-up. And she kept her hair short. She walked like a man—mostly because of her size. And with that much bulk, it'd be insanity to wear heels. She sat like a man—again, mostly because of her size. There was no way she could cross her legs. Even crossing them at the ankle—unless she worked really hard to keep her knees together …

"At least initially, they thought I was a man," she qualified, after a moment.

Right. Not for as long as it would take to get the perks.

"And I didn't want to do all that feminine shit," she added.

"So? Did you have to change your sex in order to say 'Fuck it!'? Why didn't you just change your gender?"

"Well, I did."

"Better yet, why didn't you just reject gender altogether? Become androgynous."

"Because I'm not as strong as you, okay?" She'd always been a little in awe of Kat. Her strength, her intelligence— "Nor as smart."

Kat snorted. "If I was so fucking smart, I wouldn't be here, would I?"

Dell smiled. Kat had always liked her smile too. It was so simple, so fresh, so … honest.

"I've also got dysphoria," Dell continued. "I've always felt like I was born into the wrong body."

"Born into the wrong body or born into a body you don't particularly like?"

"Both, I guess. I've never felt female. And yeah, I wish I wasn't prone to fat."

"Well, clearly you *do* feel female. Because you *are* female. You've got breasts. Or used to. You menstruate. Or used to." She'd be near or past menopause, Kat figured. "Which means you have a uterus. And even if you don't, anymore, you've got XX chromosomes. I presume. Ergo, you're female. Ergo, whatever you feel *must* be what it's like to feel female. To contort Steinem's comment about being forty."

"But it feels wrong. It's always felt wrong."

"Wrong according to what? How do you *know* it feels wrong? What's it like to 'feel *right*'?"

"It's just, I don't like— People have always told me I'm supposed to be this way or that way, and I'm not. I don't *feel* this way or that way."

"My guess is they weren't talking about sex, they were talking about gender. How you're supposed to act? What you're supposed to want?"

She nodded.

"Gender. And you *know* that!" Dell wasn't stupid. "It's not body dysphoria, it's gender rejection! And YAY! Fuck that shit! Wear whatever you want, do whatever you enjoy doing, try to become whatever you want."

"It's not that easy!"

"No, it's not, but—" Wasn't *it* easier than what Dell had gone through?

"I understand the mismatch between what's inside and what's outside," Kat said. "Really I do. I look like a middle-aged woman." She saw Dell's look. "Okay, I look like a woman on the far side of middle age. But I don't feel like a middle-aged, far side of, woman. At all. I still feel thirty. But that doesn't mean I'm going to go get a face lift. Et cetera."

"Why not? If you want to be *perceived* as thirty, and treated as thirty, because you do feel thirty …"

Good question.

"Because …"

Really good question.

"Because it's more honest to try to change people's opinions of sixty."

"And more difficult. Perhaps impossible. So …"

"Yeah."

Another easy silence followed, then Kat started chuckling.

Dell turned to her. "What?"

"Remember the OFOs?"

Dell burst out laughing. "Yes! They'd organized an Old Folks' Olympics at River Oaks. "The wheelchair sprint, the walker sprint, and the free-standing sprint …" They'd cleared one of the hallways. For the morning. Because that's how long it took for all the heats, then semi-finals, then finals.

"And the tennis ball throw," Kat giggled. "The pen toss." Those had been Dell's substitutes for the shot put and javelin.

"And the step-over!" Dell burst out with what could only be called a guffaw. It had been Kat's substitute for the high jump. The record-holder had stepped over a bar set at bath tub height. Unassisted. (Using one's cane would've made it the pole vault.)

GenJen: It didn't help that the gender dichotomy became intensified twenty-teens. It was the 1950s all over again. I remember walking into a toy store and being absolutely horrified. They may as well have had two separate stores.

> ↳ **Carol33:** Yes! Everything is colour-coded these days! My daughter was even reprimanded for drawing a couple big reindeer on a Christmas card. Her teacher suggest she draw little angels instead. I couldn't believe it.

Word: And again, it wasn't a gender dichotomy so much as a sex dichotomy: boys and girls. Not masculine and feminine.

RiseUp: But the two dichotomies were aligned, laid one on the other. Until they became one.

DrWho: Nicely put. And there's the *real* problem. One of three real problems. 1. Thinking gender is innate. 2. Thinking gender is binary. 3. Thinking gender is aligned with sex.

BigRed: And the thing is, and maybe this is a fourth problem, or maybe it's part of the third problem, gender itself is very sexualized. Especially in the case of girls/women. Have you ever seen a child beauty pageant? The expectation, the pressure, to be *beautiful* is bad enough, but they don't just make the girls look beautiful now, they make them look like hookers.

    ↳ **Shazaam:** Yeah, it's everywhere. I used to love watching *So You Think You Can Dance,* but now every women's dance looks like a pole dance. And it was such a surprise. I mean, until then— They've got a lot of brilliant choreographers and a genius costume department—

    ↳ **Abby8:** It's probably pressure from the producers. Sex it up!

    ↳ **LovesScience:** I wonder if there isn't also some bottom-up pressure going on. Earlier puberty, hormones in the food, the increase of porn ...

    ↳ **DrWho:** Cause or effect though? Well, not the hormones or puberty onset, but the increase in porn/pornification: is it a reason for the increased sexuality or a response to it?

    ↳ **ExAcademe:** Could be both.

    ↳ **BigRed:** Could also be that since sex was the tool of our subordination, men insisted we be sexed. Heavily and constantly.

    ↳ **LovesSarcasm:** *Was?*

SeeJaneScream: And then on top of all that, along comes the trans thing.

GenJen: Meaning ... ?

SeeJaneScream: Meaning transpeople *reinforce* the notion that gender has to align with sex. Otherwise, they wouldn't change sex to change gender.

BigRed: And otherwise they wouldn't call themselves 'women'.

DrWho: Right, but again, is that cause or effect? Did the trans movement reinforce the gender-sex alignment or did it flourish because of it? (I know, yes, ExAcademe, could be both.)

RadFemRocks: I find it interesting that the trans movement suggests essentialism, the notion that gender is nature, not nurture, not a social construction. And yet, at the same time, if it *was* essentialist, if feeling feminine was natural for women and feeling masculine was natural for men, then we wouldn't *have* men feeling feminine and wanting to change sex in order to express that femininity.

   ↳ **ExAcademe:** Irrational to the core.

    ↳ **TeeTee:** Follow the money.

     ↳ **ThinkAboutIt:** Please elaborate.

    ↳ **TeeTee:** I'm suggesting it's not all that irrational if you follow the money. Don't you all find it odd that 1 in 100 kids is now deemed 'transgender'? In 2003, it was 1 in 11,900 for males and 1 in 30,400 for females. That's a HUGE increase even for fifteen years.

     ↳ **LovesScience:** Huge indeed. Increases of 12,000% and 33,000% , respectively. Where are you getting those numbers from?

ↆ **TeeTee:** A study by the Johns Hopkins School of Medicine. It was published in *Journal of Clinical Endocrinology & Metabolism*. Vol.161, 2003.

ↆ **DrWho:** So are you suggesting there's been some endocrine fuck-up due to environmental, possibly food chain, factors? Same hypothesis that supposedly explains the increasingly earlier onset of puberty?

ↆ **TeeTee:** Actually, no. I didn't think of that. I was suggesting BigPharm. Not BigFarm. ☺

ↆ **ThinkAboutIt:** Do they stand to gain that much? I mean how many people are we talking about? Seeking testosterone inhibitors or estrogen shots. And surgery. Which wouldn't be BigPharm, but would at least be the medical industry.

ↆ **TeeTee:** Okay, point taken, they may not be driving the transmania, but since they benefit, they're surely supporting it.

ↆ **GenJen:** And ten years from now, there'll be class action suits by detransitioning transgenders. The drugs they're on? Depression and anxiety will be the least of their concerns. Migraines, vision problems, joint pain, respiratory problems, reduced liver function ...

ↆ **RadFemRocks:** I agree. Counsellors, parents, physicians, surgeons ... Take note.

GenJen: And sort of the flip side to RadFemRocks' comment, if gender *isn't* socially constructed—that is, if it *is* dependent on sex—how do we explain effeminate men and 'tomboys'? How is it that many males use their voice and their hands in a very expressive fashion? How is it that many females are strong and aggressive?

LovesScience: But it's not *completely* socially constructed. Which is what you were suggesting, right? Gender is a hodgepodge of personality traits and preferences, and some of those *are* biologically-based, at least to some extent.

DrWho: But not necessarily by the biology of our sex. Repeat. Some males are gentle. Some females are aggressive. Some males are fond of pastels. Some females hate them.

ExAcademe: So the problem is determining which of, and to what extent, various elements *are* determined by sex. My guess is that very little is fully determined by sex, but the problem is we'll never know because we condition according to sex as soon as the child is born.

RadFemRocks: So, first, we should get rid of gender, get rid of the arbitrary collective of attributes, because we surely haven't got it right. For example, how can we possibly know that a preference for blue goes with engineering skill? In fact, history shows that pink used to be associated with male and blue with female. Which proves that colour preference is one of the attributes in gender that's *not* genuinely sex-aligned.

Abby8: I'm with you there. Our society brainwashes us into gender. We need deprogramming.

GenJen: Yes! Read Martine Rothblatt's *The Apartheid of Sex*. She used to be Martin. Then read her later book, *Virtually Human*. Having been on both sides, she comes to the conclusion that it's all shit. Gender. The roles, the expectations, the binary.

    ↳ **LovesSarcasm:** Duh.

LovesScience: But there *are* some differences.

ThinkAboutIt: Yes, but there is also significant overlap. As Cordelia Fine explains, even for the largest difference, there's still twenty percent of women who are more male-like than the average male.

BigRed: Right, okay, so once we get rid of gender, we may find that females *tend* to have these attributes and males *tend* to have those attributes. But so what? Every tendency is going to be just that: a *tendency*. A matter of degree.

GenJen: And even if it's *not* a tendency, but a *guaranteed* difference, still, *so what?*

SeeJaneScream: Oh, *good question!*

Youngun: What about brain sex?

    ↳ **ThinkAbout It:** Read Cordelia Fine.

RadFemRocks: Is there such a thing? Maybe men in general *can* rotate objects in their minds better than women. But maybe that's because they played with Lego more. Maybe it's because they had more opportunities to navigate themselves through space. Remember that experiment with the cats in the little go-cart? The one behind the wheel learned to navigate its way around the room, but the one in the passenger seat didn't.

    ↳ **SeeJaneScream:** And guess who's expected to sit in the passenger seat?

    ↳ **Abby8:** You know, when I was growing up, I didn't even see a map of our city. It was kept in the glove compartment. Which was off-limits. Because it was car stuff. Guy stuff.

Word: Note the 'in general'!

Carol33: But isn't the brain responsible for sending chemicals through our bodies, chemicals such as testosterone and estrogen?

LovesScience: Yes, but those chemicals are *produced* by the testicles and ovaries. The brain can't send testosterone that doesn't exist.

RadFemRocks: Regardless, we should certainly be rejecting the socially constructed elements. And as BigRed points out, we're left with mere tendencies. As Word said, note the 'in general'. Which means we should also be rejecting the alignment of gender with sex. Because at best, it's only a very approximate alignment.

BigRed: With you there. One's gender isn't connected to, doesn't *have to be* connected to, one's sex! It's not a boxed set. Patti Smith. David Bowie. Prince. Gender outlaws, every one of them.

    ↳ **ExAcademe:** George Sand. Joan of Arc. Et cetera.

RadFemRocks: I'd advocate rejecting gender identity, identity based on gender. Because after you reject the sex-linked elements, what's left? Just a plain old hodgepodge of preferences and personality traits that doesn't need a name. Because they are so many combinations.

↳ **BigRed:** Yeah, my friend was diagnosed with a Gender Identity Disorder. What the fuck is that? It doesn't even make sense. Who *identifies* themselves by their *gender*?

↳ **Abby8:** A lot of people! Mr. Ms. Man. Woman.

↳ **Word:** No, those refer to sex. Not gender.

↳ **Abby8:** I dunno. I think a lot of people mean to include gender. When you hear someone say they're a man, don't you think they mean something more than just male?

↳ **SeeJaneScream:** I agree. When a guy says 'I'm a man', it sounds like 'I'm a *real* man'! A *he*-man! Which is adding gender—masculinity. *Hyper*masculinity.

↳ **Shazaam:** Same as women who identify themselves *as* women. *Real* women.

↳ **RiseUp:** *Total* women! Remember Marabel Morgan's book?

↳ **BigRed:** Oh god, yes. It was a frickin' bestseller.

↳ **GenJen:** Tell your friend to get a new doctor. Whoever made that diagnosis is out-of-date. The DSM now calls it Gender Dysphoria.

Youngun: Yeah, we need to be gender queer.

BigRed: No, that confuses gender with sexual orientation, because of the 'queer'.

Abby8: Non-binary?

Word: I like that one because it draws attention to the conception of gender as a dichotomy, an either/or. Which, surprise, is what sex is.

Abby8: Gender fluid!

RadFemRocks: But that still concedes 'gender'. Why not go all the way? Don't just make gender more flexible—eliminate it altogether. Once it's separated from sex, it makes no sense. Furthermore, it keeps women subordinated. So how about agender? Or nongendered? Or, best, no word at all.

Word: I agree. Gender adds to the differentiation between men and women. Between males and females. And why do we need to do that? (Why do people *think* we need to do that?) Because differentiation is a prerequisite for classification. *Class*-ification. We need women to be different from men in order to subordinate women to men, put them in a different, lower, class.

GenJen: Word, you're absolutely right: "Gender is a political issue and social hierarchy." I'm sure lots of people have said this, but I just read it in Barrett's *Female Erasure*—Bilek and Ceallaigh say it in their article.

    ↳ **ExAcademe:** But only the binary version aligned with sex keeps women subordinated.

    ↳ **RadFemRocks:** Granted. But, as I've said, once we get rid of that version, what's left?

BigRed: And speaking of terminology, *because* gender is a social construct, the term 'cisgender' is nonsense!

> ↳ **Word:** Well, it's not *nonsense*—because the word refers to the alignment of gender with sex, as we've been discussing.

BigRed: Okay, *idiotic* then. Or rather, anyone who is cisgender is an idiot. Anyone who thinks *at all* is—*trans*gender!

Carol33: I agree with you in theory, but in practice, some of us—and we're not idiots—*have* to be gendered. To keep our jobs.

> ↳ **Youngun:** Really? Unless you're an airline attendant or news anchor, I don't see how not wearing make-up or heels would get you fired. I mean, if it did, wouldn't you have legal recourse?

Carol33: In theory.

GenJen: In practice, the official reason for being fired might be something else, but my guess is that often it's because you're not feminine enough.

SeeJaneScream: Not feminine enough or not subordinate enough?

RadFemRocks: Same thing. See?

SeeJaneScream: Whatever, it's just another way to call us crazy. 'Us' meaning those who reject the subordination of women. Which is made so much easier *by gender*. Wear heels, have kids—both will do the trick: keep you from running the fuck away.

All right," Dr. Gagnon began, "last time we didn't get to the question I'd asked you previously to think about. What would *you* say is your gender identity? We'll need to establish that as a prerequisite for exploring your Gender Identity Disorder."

Had he not heard a word she'd said last time?

"I don't identify myself by gender," Kat said. "Nor even by sex unless I'm speaking with my physician, in a medical context. I recognize that I'm female, but as far as *I'm* concerned, that matters as much to who I am as my height, my shoe size ..."

"So how do you identify yourself? When people ask 'What are you?'"

"Well, first, I've never had anyone *ask* that question. Usually they ask 'What do you do?' And I answer *that* question," she anticipated him, "by telling the person what I do for income, since that's usually what they mean."

"But if you had to list the things that *define* you—"

"I'm a writer."

"That's it?"

"Um, I used to be an athlete of sorts. I have a passion for music. I love dogs. Are you interested in dating me?"

"What? No, I—"

"Then why does any of this matter?"

"Well, sometimes employers ask about hobbies. And they certainly, and justifiably so, want to know about your personality traits—whether you're a go-getter, a team player, that sort of thing."

"And I'd call those things hobbies and personality traits. 'Identity' is too vague. And at the same time, too specific. And regardless, sex is irrelevant. To hobbies and personality traits. Which makes gender, and gender identity, irrelevant."

"How so?" he asked, a frown on his face. As if he was seriously considering what she was saying.

"Gender presumes that sex *is* relevant. To hobbies and personality traits."

He steepled his fingers. As if he was *seriously* considering what she was saying.

"I recognize that my gender is important to *other* people," Kat continued, "but I also recognize that although a lot of people, mostly white people, *don't* identify themselves by skin colour—" she paused to think about that for a moment. Did the dominant sex class, men, identify themselves less often by sex? Because being male was the norm, so it needed no qualification, no identification?

"Is there a Racial Identity Disorder?" she asked. "For black-skinned people who don't go around identifying themselves by their skin colour?" And, or, who don't like rap music? Who want to be a neurosurgeon instead of—

"Well, certainly if a black-skinned person thought they were white-skinned, that would be an indication of dysphoria. Surely you'd agree they have a delusion, they're out of touch with reality—"

"And if I thought I were male, you could legitimately diagnose me as having a Sex Identity Disorder. Sex Dysphoria."

Her second group session, Gender Dysphoria, didn't go any better than the Anger Management group session she'd attended.

"Katherine, any thoughts?"

"Yeah. The concept of gender *dysphoria* depends on believing that gender is innate and that it matches one's sex. When it fails to do so, it's a *disorder*. But that it *can* fail to do so—isn't that proof that it's *not* innate?"

Everyone stared at her. Then at the group leader.

"Furthermore," Kat continued, "otherwise—that is, if you *don't* believe that gender is innate—then isn't the not matching just a matter of not conforming? Since when is nonconformity *a mental illness?*"

Since, she could answer her own question, mere disagreement had become insult. And *that* had happened when she was still teaching: her students ran to the Dean whenever she challenged their reasoning, saying she didn't respect their opinions. Odd that intolerance for dissent occurred at the same time everyone was screaming about inclusiveness: 'You have to accept me, and my opinions, but I don't have to accept you, yours.' Then again, she thought, it wasn't really odd: self-interest almost always trumps logical consistency.

"No, I think you misunderstand," the leader said kindly. "The mental illness is thinking you're a man."

"No, I think *you* misunderstand," Kat replied. "That would be *sex* dysphoria. And I don't have that." So she got up and walked out.

The following week, week four, Kat called Cynthia at the appointed time, fully expecting to be told she was not available. But no, she could speak to Kat now, please hold.

"Hello, Katherine?"

"Yes! I'm so glad we can talk!"

"Yes, how are you?"

"Fine. Well, not fine. I'd like to discuss … Okay," Kat jumped right in with her first question. "Fraud is defined as 'a deliberate deception to secure unfair or unlawful gain.'" She'd finally managed to do some research online. "And—"

"The way you dress—it's deliberate."

"Yes, but it's not a deliberate *deception*. The court didn't prove intent to deceive."

Cynthia seemed unmoved.

"And what unfair gain does it achieve? I'm not actually *passing* as a man, to get a certain job, for example."

"No," Cynthia paused, "but it's unfair for women to act as anything but women."

"How is that *unfair?*"

Cynthia waited. Didn't have to wait long.

"No," Kat said. In flat out denial. "You mean it's considered unfair for women to act as anything but subordinates? To men?"

Of course. It was, she saw now, a straight line from the cult of male entitlement. Some of the participants at one of the radfem sites Kat loved had hypothesized that it had started, or at least the *understanding* of it had started, when what's-his-name had cried, in the manifesto he left after his shooting spree and suicide, 'No fair!' when none of the women he'd wanted had wanted him. Kat had pointed out, however, that a 1960s sci-fi movie had portrayed the same sense of entitlement: when there weren't enough women left to 'go around', they, the men, proclaimed that every woman should be available to more than one man. It was only fair. But of course, men have felt, have *been*, entitled to women's sexuality since forever; women's history is one of sexual slavery. Men have owned them, bought and sold them, used them without consent, without pay …

But to extend sexual availability to subordination— You'd think the subordination would be established first and the sexual availability from that ... Which it was, she realized. Had been. That men considered women less important, and had done so for a very long time, was obvious. Witness the pay differentials, the status differentials, the many studies showing that men routinely interrupted women— Even the men who visited the forementioned radfem sites typically barged into the room, so to speak, then insisted on commenting at length. Usually without first reading the discussion to that point.

And so, now, she tried to wrap her head around the logic: if a woman resisted subordination, she could not be considered sexually available. Damn straight. But not fair.

Of course, it all depended on the definition of 'fair'. And men defined—everything. Still. After all.

"According to the revised Section 380(1), which addresses Fraud," Cynthia elaborated, when Kat's silence had gone on too long, "'Anyone who, by deceit, falsehood, or other fraudulent means'—the courts look for a 'dishonest act'—which they find, in cases of gender fraud—'whether or not it is a false pretence within the meaning of this Act, deprives the public or any person, whether ascertained or not, of any property, money, or valuable security, or any service' is guilty of fraud."

"Whether or not it's a false pretence?" Kat hadn't missed that. It contradicted the definition as deliberate deception. And, of course, it depended on your definition: she didn't consider wearing comfortable clothing or going without make-up to be in any way 'false'; it was only 'false' if one thought gender norms were—truly, really—aligned with sex.

"And the valuable security or service of which I'm depriving the public—I assume that means the male public—is that of subordination?"

This was insane.

"And it doesn't even have to be ascertained?" Kat hadn't missed that either. "How the hell did that clause get in there? Doesn't that amount to 'There need not be any evidence'? Of said deprivation?"

"The Supreme Court holds that deprivation is satisfied on proof of detriment," Cynthia replied. "There doesn't have to be actual loss."

"A test case has already gone before the Supreme Court?" My god, but she'd had her head in the sand. No, wait, why hadn't any of this been mentioned on any of the radfem sites? Oh. It probably had. And those sites had been censored. Or just shut down. That had started happening soon after radical feminists started objecting to transwomen calling themselves women. GenderTrender and RadFemReview had been the first to go. Then several women's Twitter accounts had been suspended. And unless there remained a site on which to publicize the censorship …

Cynthia spelled it out. "Dismantling sexism—which gender fraud does—is to the detriment of males."

Right. In a nutshell.

"And as for the adverse consequences that need to be shown in cases of fraud," she continued, "men lose all the privileges they've traditionally had, because of their sex, their gender."

"But they're not the same! I'm not posing as *male*!"

"Kat, they've been the same since …"

Since the trans shit hit the fan. Since all the Gender Recognition legislation. The early twenty-teens.

"Gender fraud is a generalized version of identity theft," Cynthia said. "Women who appear and act masculine are stealing men's identity."

Right, Kat thought. Because men identify *as* men. As *masculine*. Gender fraud depended on gender identity.

"Okay, you said 'Deprivation is satisfied on proof of detriment'—what about detriment *to women?*"

Cynthia was silent.

Kat suddenly saw a door *wide open.* "Surely this insistence on female subordination—it must be considered a violation of human rights!"

"It would be … if women were considered, by the courts, to be human."

Ah. Porn. MacKinnon and Dworkin. Of course women were human. Until honoring their human rights violated men's human rights.

So there it was. Even if Kat could somehow convince her psychiatrist that she was not suffering 'serious mental deterioration' and so avoid getting her six months renewed, they could still get her on 'danger to others': she was a danger to others—that is, men—simply by rejecting gender. Femininity was, after all, as Lierre Keith put it, "a set of behaviors that are in essence ritualized submission." And said submission was, apparently, essential to men.

She could challenge their definition of 'danger' and/or whether the danger she posed justified incarceration, but that sounded like a class action suit. Okay, so maybe they could …

"What we can do," Cynthia said, "is try to obtain a conversion to a community treatment order."

That got Kat's interest. "What does that mean, exactly?"

"First, your psychiatrist has to determine that you meet the criteria for a community treatment order, then a treatment plan is developed in consultation with other health care workers, social workers, family members, a substitute decision maker—"

"I don't have—"

"Then you follow the plan while living in the community. Failure to do so would result in readmission."

"What would the plan involve?"

"That depends. Probably weekly meetings with someone, proving that you're complying. With gender expectations."

Shit. Well, better to pretend once a week, and even whenever she went into town, than every second of the day. Far better. She'd have the forest. Every day. The lake. Every day. Her cabin.

"Okay, yes, let's do that. Please."

That night, as they were getting ready for bed— Well, as Holly was getting ready for bed. Kat just—got into her bed. Though she now had to wash off what little make-up she'd put on. But Holly was at her vanity fastidiously applying some sort of cream to her face, paying careful attention to the corners of her eyes and the hollows under her eyes …

Kat asked her whether she'd ever tried to get a community order.

Holly snorted. "Your lawyer advise that?" She put aside the magazine she'd been flipping through. *Cosmopolitan.* A far cry from *Today's Fire Fighter.* Or *The Journal of …*

"Yeah."

"Waste of time." She continued to massage the cream into her skin. "Why?"

"Your psychiatrist needs to sign off on it."

"Yeah, and … ?"

"Don't you get it?" She turned to her. "Every psychiatrist here is a male chauvinist pig."

Kat grinned. She hadn't heard that phrase since the 70s. Now, she supposed such men would be called an MRA. A men's rights advocate. She liked male chauvinist pig better.

"Who else would apply for such a position?" Holly asked, then turned back to her mirror.

Good point.

"Yeah, but they've still gotta follow the rules, right?"

Holly didn't respond.

"I was thinking maybe … Six months is a long time."

Holly didn't respond.

"How long have you been here? So far?"

Holly didn't respond.

"Holly?"

"Two years."

Next morning, Kat watched Holly put on her make-up. Imitated her, step by infuriating step. The end result was not even close. She wiped herself clean and started over. You can do this, she told herself. You've got this.

That she had truly gone down the rabbit hole became clear to her the following week when she picked up a pamphlet on the table in the outer room of her psychiatrist's office and started reading: "From a medical and scientific standpoint, there is no such thing as a transgender person; all humans are either biologically male or female." Yes! She read on. "Individuals who maintain they are trapped in bodies of the wrong gender are suffering from delusions and their distress is purely psychological." Yes, again! Well, except for "*bodies* of the wrong *gender*"— "The appropriate treatment for such a case is mental health care, not sex-change surgery that reinforces a mental disorder rather than treating it." Another yes! Well, yes to the not sex-change surgery. Not yes to the mental health care.

"There is no reason to grant special rights to people who call themselves transgender"—definite yes here!—"and laws that include protections for 'gender identity' and 'gender expression' are dangerous to society." STANDING OVATION!

The pamphlet was written by Thaddeus Baklinksi. A staff writer for a *conservative Christian* group. She was a staunch atheist. Had been since her late teens. How was it she agreed so whole-heartedly with a group that was not only Christian, but conservative? Well, not *whole*-heartedly, because they'd mixed up gender and sex, and they called a 'misalignment' of the two a mental disorder requiring mental health care. Still. She agreed that sex-change surgery wasn't necessary if you simply didn't accept the gender assigned to your sex.

She didn't have to wait long for her surprise to be … nullified. She simply read on: "Male and female, He created them." Well, not in the other version of Genesis. "What God has made, let no man put asunder." Or woman, if he'd thought us worth acknowledgement. "And men shall be men and women shall be women." And there it was. A new commandment. Apparently.

"I heard you walked out of group yesterday. Again." He'd tilted his head to look at her, as if considering some strange creature he had yet to figure out.

"Yes." She sighed. "It was the wrong group. We've been over this," she added. "I don't have sex dysphoria. And gender dysphoria is just ignoring sex-aligned social conventions. Not mental illness."

"But the purpose of group, all the groups, is to help you!"

"Help me how? Help me do what?"

"Well," he stuttered, "help you conform to gender expectations."

So he admitted it was all about conforming. No matter.

"I don't need any help conforming to gender expectations. I'm perfectly capable of doing that on my own, if I so choose," she said. Not mentioning her inability to walk on stilt shoes. "But I do *not* so choose. Is that a crime?"

He let a moment pass. "I think you know the answer to that."

"Yes," she sighed. Would have stared out the window if there'd been one. "*Why* is it a crime? Can you try to help me understand that?"

"Well," he replied, missing her sarcasm, "a society functions best when people conform to certain roles."

"Roles accorded by sex?"

He nodded. "Among others."

Hm.

"It functions best *for men*, you mean. When people conform to roles accorded by sex."

He didn't respond.

"Because without that caveat, the evidence is against you."

Again, he didn't respond. To ask what she meant would be to put himself in a position of relative weakness. To a woman, no less. Can't have that.

"Most societies have had roles accorded by sex," she elaborated. "And most people in most societies have conformed to those roles. But they have not functioned well. At all."

She waited. Nope. He was simply *not* going to ask.

"Most such societies have been characterized by a high level of violence by men. That alone argues against your claim. But in addition, most such societies have denied basic human rights to women. The right to vote. The right to an education. The right to reproductive control. Freedom of movement. Health, safety." She anticipated. "Consider assault and battery, rape, femicide."

A long silence filled the room.

"Well, be that as it may," he finally said, "you are here, now, and it's in your best interests to at least *try*."

Try what exactly, he didn't say. But his point was a good one. It wouldn't be enough to simply *attend* all the classes and groups. She had to— What? Behave appropriately. Speak appropriately. Say nice shit or keep her mouth shut.

RiseUp: What bothers me is that even feminists, *so-called* feminists, are wearing make-up these days. What's next, a feminist cheerleading squad?

    ↳ **LovesSarcasm:** Feminist pole-dancers.

BigRed: Proof that it's become normalized. To sexualize your appearance for the male gaze.

    ↳ **Youngun:** What are you talking about? I wear make-up and it's not to "sexualize my appearance for the male gaze"!

        ↳ **BigRed:** Okay, why do you do it?

    ↳ **Youngun:** I don't know, it's what women do!

        ↳ **BigRed:** Yes, but *why* is that what women do? *Why* do *you* do it?

    ↳ **Youngun:** I don't know, to look nice, I guess.

        ↳ **RiseUp:** That's twice now you've said you don't know. Don't you think you *should* know why you do what you do? Dig a little deeper. Figure it out.

⤷ **BigRed:** Don't you see? The make-up, the short tight skirt, the heels— It all screams 'Fuck me!' And what do you think's going to happen when you scream 'Fuck me!' all day? To your opportunities, your treatment?

⤷ **SeeJaneScream:** And a 'plunging' neckline points like an arrow to breasts that are likely padded and pushed up—is it any wonder you find yourself saying "My eyes are up here"? Talk about a mixed message.

RadFemRocks: And not just *your* opportunities, *your* treatment. It hurts us all. To the extent that people, especially men, overgeneralize, your appearing sexual all the time makes them think of us *all* as sexual. All the time.

RiseUp: And given the time and energy/effort all those things take, men will expect us *all* to spend a lot of time and energy/effort to please them.

⤷ **RadFemRocks:** Yes! And when one of us doesn't, well, hell hath no fury like a man ignored by women.

RiseUp: And the heels, the waxing, the surgeries—to plump up our breasts and buttocks, to prettify our vulva, to tighten our vagina—it says we're willing to *endure pain* if it pleases men.

⤷ **RadFemRocks:** And what the fuck for? *What have they done for us lately?*

ExAcademe: So many of us are complicit in our own subordination. Not only do we, by wearing make-up, emphasize our sexuality, *as a matter of daily routine*, we endorse the importance of our appearance and, since we cover our wrinkles and grey hair, the importance of youth over age. We speak in a higher register than is actually necessary, which also makes us come across as child-like and thus more easily dismissed. We smile more often than we need to and thus cancel the importance of our words.

SeeJaneScream: Yes! We shouldn't do *any* of that.

BigRed: And we shouldn't expect a man to pay our way for anything. Only invalids and children need to have someone else pay their way.

   ↳ **Carol33:** But my boyfriend makes so much more than me. I think it's only fair that he pay sometimes.

      ↳ **BigRed:** But if, when, he does, his making more than you, and your making less, is considered *justified!* The old 'breadwinner' argument.

      ↳ **RiseUp:** Don't even accept his paying your way because you think he's just being nice. He's not paying your way to be nice. He's paying your way to express his superiority—just watch how angry he gets when you insist on paying *his* way— and to underscore your need for him, your dependence on him.

BigRed: And don't get married for the badge of maturity. It makes it that much harder for those of us who see marriage as the sexist trap it is.

   ↳ **GenJen:** Yes! Badge of maturity indeed! An unmarried woman is treated like some kind of perpetual teenager who hasn't yet grown up.

RadFemRocks: And unless you really like kids—did you want to become a nursery school teacher?—don't have them. It too is a badge of maturity and your endorsement of that irrationality makes it that much harder for those of us who choose to be child-free to be seen as adults.

RiseUp: It's also a trap. In fact, in our society, there is no stronger, no more complete, trap into subordination. Because then you *will* need him. Then you *will* become dependent on him. Which will triple his power over you. Because look, you can't take your infant to work with you, so you *will* need someone to look after it while you're out earning rent, and that will cost, probably as much, or almost as much, as you make, so you *still* won't have rent ...

BigRed: Better to form an alliance with another mother; you can work eight hours at your job while she looks after yours and hers, then she can work eight hours at her job while you look after hers and yours.

   ↳ **SeeJaneScream:** Remember the tv show *Kate and Allie?*

   ↳ **RadFemRocks:** Yes! *Great* show!

SeeJaneScream: And kids make you vulnerable. Oh so vulnerable to threat, to blackmail, in all its subtle forms.

Hey, whatcha' doin'?" Dell sat down heavily beside Kat. She was in the common room, in the corner, away from the always-on and always-irritating tv, flipping through the magazine in her hands. Putting in time until three o'clock.

"Reading a magazine." Not a journal of philosophy. "That's what women do, right?" She was trying.

"Yeah … but that's not reading."

Kat was practically tearing the pages.

"Okay, I'm trying to find just one image of a woman standing with both feet, bare feet, flat on the ground."

"Good luck." Dell picked up another magazine from the low table in front of them.

"Indeed. Every single picture, especially the ones actually showing women in bare feet, show them putting all of their weight on just one leg. Off-balance. The foot of the other leg is raised." She turned a few pages. "Sometimes the other *leg* is raised. Off the ground. God knows why."

"Or," Dell held her magazine open to Kat, "she's standing on tippy-toe."

"Yeah," Kat looked at the picture Dell was showing her, "who does that? Except when you're reaching for the something on the top shelf of the kitchen cupboard."

"I do it all the time. I like to pretend I'm a little girl."

Kat burst out laughing. "But little girls— *I* never walked on tippy-toe when I was a little girl."

"Actually, neither did I," Dell said, thinking about it.

Kat turned another page.

"And speaking of which, cupboards and counters et cetera should be six inches lower. I mean, if women are supposed to stay in the kitchen, they should at least make them our size. You know what I mean," she added.

Dell nodded, and continued leafing through the magazine she'd picked up.

"Maybe they've worn heels so much, their Achilles tendons are too short to enable flat-foot standing."

Kat looked at her. Was she serious? Maybe. In which case, women were idiots.

"Or maybe the photographer, a man, tells them how to stand," Dell tossed out another suggestion.

"And they listen."

Dell nodded. "To keep the job. To get paid."

Kat considered that. "They should go on strike. Refuse any pose that's demeaning to women. Refuse— No, that would cover it."

"There's a website ... Someone's photographed men in women's poses from ads ... Or no, maybe it's reversals of comic book images ... Anyway, it's hilarious. Not to mention enlightening."

"I'll bet."

After a few more moments, Dell checked her watch. It was three.

"So, shall we 'take the air'?"

"Oh god," Kat said, "do they really call it that? That sounds so ... eighteenth century. How far back do they intend to take us?"

"To Salem."

Once they were outside, Kat noticed that Dell was wearing a pair of Reeboks.

"Hey, you've got a pair of running shoes!"

"No, running shoes aren't allowed. As you know. *Should* know. These are *walking* shoes. Said so on the box, brought by a friend."

"Ah. I see. They're very nice. Walking shoes."

They started walking slowly around the perimeter of the yard, Kat resisting the urge to speed up a little.

"So what's it like being male?" Kat opened, asking a question she'd been saving for just such a moment. "Or, rather, having male hormones? I mean, there's no way I can know which parts of how I feel are due to being female and which parts are due to just being human in the way that I am."

Dell turned to grin at Kat and regretted not having cultivated an outside-of-work friendship with Kat back when.

"How I feel could be related to my levels of estrogen and progesterone," Kat explained, "but it could instead, or also, be related to my levels of dopamine and vasopressin, for example. How could I know which of what I feel is due to what? Just like one doesn't know what it feels like to be healthy until one's been sick. But you—you're in a privileged epistemological state—"

"*That's* what this is!" Dell gestured at her body, from her stubbled and badly made-up face down along her flowered polyester dress to her new Reeboks.

Kat gave a lop-sided smile, then continued. "So you know what's due to being female and what's due to being male. Because you've been both. So ... what's it like to be male? What's been different about your personality, your experience of things, since you've been taking testosterone? I mean now that you've got ten times the testosterone coursing through your body …"

"Most of the time it feels good," Dell said. "*Really* good," she smiled. "I feel stronger, I feel more confident, I have more energy. I don't cry as easily."

"But—"

"But—and this is going to sound really strange—I don't think as much."

Kat snorted. "Really?"

Dell nodded. "I think it might have something to do with having more energy, needing to be more active, more on the move. You become less … introspective."

"Interesting. *Very* interesting." Kat thought about that. The repercussions of that.

"They really should be doing studies of people who've transitioned," she concluded. "In-depth studies. Maybe, finally, we'd be able to figure out which differences are due to sex, to nature, and which to nurture."

They walked on.

"Are you more aggressive?" she asked.

"Yeah."

Kat grinned. Dell had never been a talkative person. Say what you mean, mean what you say, then shut the fuck up. It was one of the things Kat had liked about her.

"More violent?"

"Maybe."

She was. Kat could tell. She just didn't want to admit it.

"I feel more calm."

"Isn't that a contradiction?"

"No, I think it's connected to the not crying as easily. Emotionally, I'm more …"

"Please don't say 'stable'."

"Flat."

"Hm." Kat considered the difference. "Anything else?"

"Well, there's the physical stuff. My bones hurt sometimes. More than they used to. And although I didn't lose very much fat, I did gain muscle. So overall I'm heavier. That's a bitch. I thought I'd become leaner."

"So are you at a greater risk of having a heart attack?"

She shrugged. "Maybe."

"You don't know? Your doctor hasn't told you?"

She shook her head.

"Had you planned to get bottom surgery?"

"No. No point. It's not like anyone's gonna see me naked. What they see, now, is male; that's enough for me."

Kat nodded. "Probably cost a lot anyway."

"Oh, it'd be covered."

"By Bayside's plan?"

"No, by the government."

"Really?" Kat considered that. "So my taxes helped pay for …" She shut her mouth. She'd always thought that cosmetic surgery wasn't covered. And rightly so. She wished that lifestyle-induced medical care wasn't covered either. Why should she pay for someone's bypass surgery when it was caused by a lazy lifetime of burgers and donuts? So … sex change surgery wasn't considered cosmetic. But it was surely just an issue of appearance, wasn't it? She'd have to think about that. Good thing she was female. And could. She grinned to herself.

They finished the lap around the yard in companionable silence.

"Hang on," Dell suddenly stopped. "I've gotta sit for bit." She headed to the nearby bench, somewhat unsteadily.

"Are you okay?" Kat was alarmed.

"No. They've got me on some heavy-duty diet pills. So I'm nauseous most of the time, and dizzy, and I've got a headache that hasn't gone away for a week …" She almost collapsed onto the bench.

"How's your blood pressure?"

"Through the roof, no doubt."

"Well, fuck that."

"Yeah. How?"

Kat was silent. How indeed.

"Keep talking," Dell said, panting a little. "What were you going to ask next?"

"Is male privilege all it's thought to be? By women?"

"Pretty much, yeah. I'm taken seriously now." Dell paused. As much for breath as for further thought. "What I think, what I want, what I do— It all *counts* more now. Even though it hasn't changed."

Kat nodded. She could understand that. No question.

"My female body doesn't get in the way of my aspirations," Dell added. "It doesn't ghettoize me."

Kat nodded again. And was relieved to see that Dell's physical distress was diminishing.

"And," Dell grinned broadly as she turned to Kat, "you have no idea what it's like to feel like the norm."

Kat stared at her. How perfectly said. She recalled Andrea Dworkin's comment that in a male supremacist society—she preferred that description to patriarchy, for its lack of 'fatherly'— the *male* condition is taken to be the *human* condition, so when a man says something, he's not dismissed as having some special bone to pick.

"You'd love it, even for just one goddamned minute," Dell added. "Let alone a whole day. A week. A month. Years."

Yes, she would. The effect that would have. Would have had. Years of not always being set aside in some little box …

"And changing sex has made it easier to act on my preferences."

Yeah. She got that. Because of other people. They could open or close doors. And they did so on the basis of how they perceived you. Which included, unfortunately, what sex they perceived you to be. When one's preferences were contrary to the straitjacket imposed by idiots and assholes … Straitjacket determined not only by sex, but also by height, skin color, attractiveness …

"But changing your sex implies you've accepted the binary nature of gender," Kat said.

"No, it just implies that I gave up. It got so … exhausting. Challenging gender. Every day. Every minute of every day."

Yeah. She got that too. Wasn't that why she became a hermit?

"Too bad you couldn't just live in drag. I mean present as a male without having to take the testosterone."

"Yeah, and if I could have gotten away with that, close-up, I would have. But that would imply accepting the binary nature of gender too."

"True."

Dell heaved herself up off the bench, and seemed ready for another lap. Kat hesitated.

"It's okay. I'm okay now."

"Okay. But stop when you need to."

"Will do."

After a few minutes of companionable silence, Kat asked another question she'd been wondering about.

"So do you regret it?"

"Sometimes. People really resent a woman trying to be a man."

Kat nodded.

"Remember that movie about Teena Brandon?" Dell asked.

"But you're still alive."

"Yeah, but I've received threats. And I'm here."

"Yeah how did that happen?"

"I suspect one of my male subordinates reported me. Figured it out. Then got tired of not only having a woman as the boss of him, but a woman who thought she was a man. There was such a feeling of … hostility, sure, but also … resentment, maybe."

"No surprise. Even tomboys are resented. Guys resent you for trying to muscle in on their territory, and women resent you for being above yourself. They've accepted their subordinate position in society, why shouldn't you?"

"They should do studies about that too. Resentment toward tomboys."

"Yeah but girls aren't worthy subjects of study," Kat said. "Look how long it took to realize that heart attacks in women have different symptoms than in men."

Dell headed to the next bench and sat down. Kat was relieved.

"Any other reasons for regret?"

"Yeah. People think—people like me," Dell corrected herself, "think it'll be easier, living in a male body. But it's not. I've cut back on the testosterone. I didn't like feeling … *driven* all the time."

Kat nodded.

"And socially … I used to be called a cunt. Now I'm called a sissy. When I don't fight."

Kat nodded. "It's easier to be masculine when female," Kat said, "than to be feminine when male."

"Maybe," Dell replied. "But either way—"
"Yeah."

Next day, when Kat saw Dell enter the cafeteria at lunch, she waved her over to join her and Holly.

"Dell, Holly," she introduced them to each other as soon as Dell sat down. "Holly, Dell."

They nodded to each other.

"So how do you two know each other?" Dell asked, stabbing a chunk of lettuce with her fork.

"Holly used to be a phys-ed teacher," Kat said. "She was on a long-term placement at one of the high schools here when I was asked to cover for an English teacher with some chronic health issue."

"Widdifield. The high school," Holly said. "And Ms. Jennet. Rheumatoid arthritis."

"I'm impressed," Kat said, smiling at her.

"And what do you do now?" Dell asked Holly.

"Nothing at the moment." She proceeded to give Dell a short version of her employment history, then asked, "How did you two meet?"

Kat told her.

"And you still work there?" Holly asked Dell.

"No, I'm a Director at Bayside. It's—"

"I know it. My father was there for a while. He liked it."

"That's good to hear."

Just then, Kat saw Liz enter the cafeteria and waved her over as well. The more, the merrier, she figured. Conversation with Holly had been strained for weeks; the ease and pleasure of their initial 'catch-up' conversations had not been repeated.

"Holly, Dell, Liz. Liz, Holly, Dell." They all smiled at each other as Liz joined their table.

"And how do you two know each other?" Dell asked.

"Dr.—Kat was my professor," Liz explained. "Social Ethics."

Dell laughed as she turned to Kat. "See what you do? You get your students committed to mental institutions."

Liz answered Dell's next question about what she did now, then they focused on their food for a while.

"That's all you're eating?" Kat asked Dell, who'd finished her small salad before everyone else was even halfway through what they'd gotten.

Dell nodded. "It is if I ever want to get out of here."

"But—"

"It's not feminine to be fat."

"But it is. At least it's feminine to *have* fat. Muscle is masculine."

"It's not feminine to be *large*," Dell corrected herself.

"Ah. Right. You take up too much space." Only men are allowed to take up space. She recalled the 'manspreading' phenomenon that became so obnoxious women had to launch a poster campaign reminding men to *share* the seats on public transit.

"We all take up too much space," she added. In so many ways …

"But," she turned to Dell, "is it working? I mean, you've always been large." Dell's big and soft body was the polar opposite of Holly's compact and hard body. "I'm sure you've tried diets before."

She nodded. "Yes. And no," she added, "it's not working. It never does."

"Have my orange, at least," Kat held it out to her. She'd optimistically added it to her tray, but she knew she wouldn't eat it. Her appetite hadn't really returned.

"Okay." Dell accepted it and started peeling.

"There's a lot of people here," Kat observed, looking around the large cafeteria. She'd thought there'd been a lot when she'd first arrived, and she'd hoped that, over time, she'd become a little more comfortable with so many people, but that hadn't happened. And there seemed to be more and more women at the facility every day. Few of whom seemed mentally ill, as far as Kat was concerned.

Liz nodded. "It's pretty much full to capacity. I've heard that new ones are being built."

"Hm. I guess it's a good time to be a mental health professional."

"And I imagine stock in pharmaceutical companies is on the increase," Holly said.

Liz nodded. "If any of you have a few thousand dollars lying around, I know someone who knows about that stuff. Buying and selling stock."

Kat and Holly snorted. Dell did not, Kat noticed.

"I take it the men are in a different ward somewhere?" Kat asked.

"Yes," Liz replied, "though of course there are far fewer of them."

"Why 'of course'? I mean I can see that for gender dysphoria. Society is far harder on feminine men than on masculine women. Well, until now. But what about all the other, the legitimate, mental illnesses? The psychoses, the schizophrenia, the depression, the OCD …?"

"Women in general are more prone to be crazy," Holly grimaced. "Don't you know?"

"Oh right," Kat replied. Women who were violent, women who were angry, women who spoke their mind, women who dared to disagree with a man—they were all called crazy. A woman who wanted sex? A nymphomaniac. And one who didn't? Frigid.

"Yeah, why is that?" Dell asked. "Why is it that when women don't fit the gender straightjacket, they're called crazy, but when men don't fit the gender straightjacket, they're just called names?"

No one had an answer.

"Interesting that the names they're called are pussy, sissy, bitch ...," Kat said. "Indications of the feminine."

"They're also called fags," Liz added.

"True."

"It's men that make us crazy," Holly suggested. "Legitimately crazy. Trying to negotiate their demands, their rules, their expectations."

"And religion," Liz offered.

"Yeah, and what sex is the Pope?" Holly asked. "The Bishop? All the priests and ministers and rabbis? God himself?"

"Point taken."

"As for society being harder on feminine men," Dell circled back, "transmen have always had it harder than transwomen. They kill us, but they open the doors of every women's space for them."

"Good point," Kat said. "I wonder why that is. Was."

"Maybe because the 'they' is different," Liz offered. "I mean it's men who kill transmen, right? But it's been women—okay, some women—and people in power who—"

"Who are men," Kat saw it then.

"Okay, but why do men want transwomen to invade women's spaces?" Dell asked.

"To deprive them, women, of their spaces."

"Ah."

"And since transwomen are really still men," Holly suggested, "if they want access to women's spaces—"

"So essentially," Kat summed up, "the explanation is that whatever men want, men get." Even when they're women.

The four of them stared at their empty plates.

"So you're here for Gender Fraud too?" Holly asked Dell a few moments later.

She nodded. "And Gender Dysphoria. Personality disorder."

"Right," Holly understood. "If you're confident and competitive, and you're a woman, you must have a personality disorder."

"And you?" she looked at Liz.

"Gender Fraud. And Gender Dysphoria. And Causing a Disturbance. I was living openly as a lesbian. A butch lesbian."

"Isn't Causing a Disturbance for things that disturb the peace? Ah." Dell had the answer to her own question. "Anything that disrupts the patriarchy disturbs the peace. *Men's* peace. *Straight* men's peace."

"Causing a Disturbance also includes indecent exhibition," Liz added.

"How indecent of you to kiss a woman in public," Dell smiled. "Whereas men, straight men, can—"

"Do pretty much anything they want," Kat said. "To women. In public." Because porn was pretty much public. Now.

SeeJaneScream: But don't you think they went too far with Local Law
No.3?

Carol33: What's Local Law No.3?

SeeJaneScream: It's a law that makes illegal the intentional or
repeated refusal to use an individual's preferred name, pronoun, or
title. For example, repeatedly calling a transgender 'woman' 'him' or
'Mr.' after 'she' has made clear which pronouns and title 'she' uses."

  ↳ **Abby8:** Seriously? That's *illegal*? Where is this?

    ↳ **SeeJaneScream:** New York. Specifically, the New York City
    Commission on Human Rights, Legal Enforcement Guidance
    on Discrimination on the Basis of Gender Identity or
    Expression: Local Law No. 3 (2002) NYC Admin Code 8-
    102(23).

RadFemRocks: Pity the law didn't make it illegal to use *any* sex-
identifying pronoun or title. Why in the hell do we need one pronoun
for males and another for females? Why do we need to go around
identifying people by their sex every time we open our mouths? We
should have adopted *ze* and *zir* back in the 70s when we first started
thinking about all this. Instead we went just part of the way with *Ms.*

DrWho: That law insists we lie. Because MtFs simply *aren't* women. Even if the man gets estrogen injections, breast construction surgery, penis-into-vulva surgery, and what have you. He'll never have functioning breasts. He'll never have a functioning clitoris. He'll never have ovaries. He'll never have a uterus. Most importantly, he'll never have XX chromosomes. Because even women who've had mastectomies, clitoredectomies, and/or hysterectomies are still female.

↳ **RiseUp:** And even if he *did* somehow acquire all that, unless he got it all pretty much at birth, he'd never have the lifetime of treatment *as* a woman which, try as we do to make it not so, constructs us to some extent.

↳ **DrWho:** But again, that's gender, not sex.

BigRed: Friend of mine got arrested for that last week. Carries a fine of up to $250,000.

↳ **Carol33:** But that's insane!

LovesSarcasm: Could a guy be fined up to $250,000 fine for calling me 'Cunt'? After I've made it clear that I don't prefer or use that name?

Kat slouched in the chair across from Dr. Gagnon. "I understand you're having trouble accepting your femininity."

Good thing she'd decided not to use her make-up as war paint.

And then, trouble? Accepting? *My* femininity? She didn't know what to address first.

"You're failing all of your classes," he continued, "and you've walked out of every group session you've attended."

They're giving grades?

"Only two," she said in her defence. "I've walked out of only two sessions."

"You've attended only two."

Okay, yeah. But.

"In five weeks."

Okay, yeah.

Wait, it's been only five weeks?

"I've been told that you're refusing to take your estrogen supplements."

"*My* estrogen supplements?"

He just nodded.

She could play that game too. So she didn't say anything.

"Can you tell me why?" he asked after a long silence.

"Why I don't want to take estrogen supplements? Sure. I'm not keen to have nausea, leg cramps, or headaches. And, after five years, an increased risk of stroke and heart disease."

"But the benefits—"

"I don't mind if my skin looks its age. As for osteoporosis, I'd rather keep walking a couple hours a day. And what the fuck do I need a moist vagina for?"

He smiled.

What?

"Besides, I'm here for *gender* dysphoria. Not *sex* dysphoria. You have no mandate to address any sexual elements."

"Except that we understand refusal to take estrogen to *indicate* gender dysphoria."

Of course they did.

"How so?"

"Because every woman *has* estrogen! It's what *makes* her a woman."

"It's what makes her a female," Kat clarified. "Though you surely know that men have estrogen too."

No response.

"In any case, that's sex," she sighed. "Not gender."

No response.

"Furthermore, even if the refusal to take estrogen indicated gender dysphoria, what are you saying? If we take away the symptom, we'll have cured the illness?"

She stopped herself from pointedly looking to the wall for a diploma.

"Besides which, I *have* estrogen. Just not nearly as much as I did before menopause. And I'm still a woman. That is, I'm still a female human being. I've never contested that. You have no need to treat me in that regard." Around and around.

"Still, we'd like very much for you to take the supplements."

"Still, I'd like very much not to."

He sighed. She was *such* a recalcitrant child.

"Has it ever occurred to you," she said, trying to keep the disdain out of her voice, "that a lot of women *enjoy* menopause? Look *forward* to not being driven by their sexuality, not being *defined* by their sexuality? Look forward to saying 'Enough with that shit!'?"

He stared at her. Guess that was her answer.

"But it's like you're not even making an effort to be attractive."

"Well I tried putting a sunset and some sparkles on my cheek, but— Attractive to who?"

"Well, just, to ... look nice."

"I repeat, to who?"

He didn't answer.

"I look nice enough to me."

"Yes, well, I suppose I mean to others."

"To men?"

"Well, yes."

"But I'm not interested in looking attractive to men. You mean *sexually* attractive, right?"

"Well, I suppose—"

"I'm not interested in being sexually attractive. Because I'm not interested in being sexual. I'm not interested in reproduction."

"But surely the pleasure— Of sexual intercourse—"

"First, if I *did* engage in sexual interaction, sexual *intercourse* would be low on my list of preferred engagements. Second, there are so many *greater* pleasures. Measured by, let's use Bentham, intensity, duration, certainty, propinquity, fecundity, purity, and extent."

"But," he stammered, "sex is ... fundamental."

"No, it's not. I'm proof. Apart from a ten-year period thirty years ago, I've lived an asexual life. An extremely happy asexual life."

He didn't believe it. The look on his face said so.

"I have an idea."

Wonderful.

"It will surely sound silly to you, but given your difficulty, I think it's worth a shot. When you write, I'd like you to dot your I's with little hearts."

She stared at him. He couldn't be serious.

"Sometimes," he hastened to explain, "how you act on the outside changes how you feel on the inside. The way you write— It's very masculine."

When had he seen her writing? There must have been some intake form she'd had to fill out ... that had more than boxes to check.

"No, it's not," she disagreed. Her writing was small, very compressed, very economical. No unnecessary flourishes. It was the result of having a lot to say, all at once, and in a very small space. Initially, the margins of her school notebooks.

"Men are arrogant," she explained, "very full of themselves. They take up a lot of space. They write large." She'd seen many a man's signature. Most were huge. Laughably overconfident.

Furthermore, "You think that's how women write? With little hearts above their I's? That's how teenaged girls write. *Some* teenaged girls." She herself certainly hadn't written that way when she was a teenager. "So are you suggesting that women remain teenagers?"

Yes, that's exactly what he was suggesting. He was trying to infantilize her. It was one of the many ways women were kept subordinate.

He sighed. She was *such* a recalcitrant child. "Well, why don't we try it?"

We? But what the hell, if it meant she could get paper and pen, she'd dot her I's with little hearts.

But before she could agree, he spoke again.

"Even so, now— I get the feeling you're not taking this seriously. I've received reports and, well, it seems you're not even shaving your legs."

She stared at him for a long moment.

"BigAg is forcing farmers to use sterile seed. Up to 700 barrels of oil have been pouring into the Gulf of Mexico since 2004 because of an 'oil spill'. Carbon dioxide at 400 parts per million— the so-called point of no return because it tips the first domino in a long line of dominos whose fall then becomes inevitable and, for the most part, the effects are irreversible—causes an increase in temperature, which causes an increase in the melting of polar ice, as well as the frequency and severity of storms, which causes flooding, droughts, and infrastructure damage, resulting in reduced food, water, and energy, along with changes in disease vectors. We passed that point of no return years ago. Life as we have known it is ending.

"And you're worried about whether or not I shave my legs."

Lose the battle to win the war, Kat muttered to herself as she stood outside the door to her next group session. Lose the battle to win the war ... She entered the room and took a seat. Lose the battle to win the war ...

"Good morning, everyone!" Another bright voice, this one brimming with sympathy. Kat was already sour about having to attend the Childless Group. Now, she—

"Anne, Bethany, Shovaughn, and Katherine, welcome! I'd

like to ask each of you the question I ask everyone who comes to our group. What does 'barren' mean to you? Katherine?"

Okay, this was easy. "Nothing's growing."

"Good, and how does that make you feel?"

"Um … I don't understand the question." Be nice. That was borderline rude. Go figure.

"How does it feel to be barren?" she said gently.

"I don't know." I'm not acreage. "I guess it makes me feel empty." Yes! There you go! You lied! Yay!

"Can you elaborate?"

Lazy, lazy, lazy.

"You mean about what's it been like not having kids?"

I've been unencumbered. When I think of a woman with children, I imagine her with one in her arms, another on her back, a third clinging to her leg— She can hardly move, she's so weighted down.

"Yes."

"Well, if I'd had kids, I'd have grand-kids by now." Nicely ambiguous, she thought. And smiled. That would be more challenging than lying.

"And they can bring such joy, can't they?"

Yay for ambiguity! Because god, no. She hated kids. They were immature. By definition. So needy, so demanding.

"Katherine?"

Be nice, she told herself. Lose the battle …

So she nodded. Kept her mouth shut.

Most people had no idea how nice she was whenever she interacted with them. How much unflattering honesty she withheld.

There was nothing wrong with being immature. When you're a kid. It's just that that's why she didn't like them. She didn't like snakes either, because they were wriggly.

And being immature, they were dependent. She didn't want people depending on her. She wanted to be able to do whatever she wanted to do. Or at least to *try* to do whatever she wanted to do.

People called that selfish. (Yes, she'd had this conversation before. Many times.) But 'selfish' is self-interest *at another's expense.* Who was she hurting by being independent?

It's as if sacrifice is expected, required, the default ethical standard. At least for women.

Just a matter of time before they're reprimanded for keeping both of their kidneys. Both of their corneas.

"All right, let's move on, shall we? Anne? How do *you* feel? Not having kids."

"I feel like a failure," she admitted.

"But—" Kat caught herself in time. Shut her mouth again. Smiled. Did anyone buy it?

But, she was about to say, that's so illogical. You have no voluntary control over your reproductive system, beyond the choice to have or not have intercourse—and that's often not in your control either. It would be like feeling like a failure because you're not blond.

"Shovaughn? Let's hear from you."

"I feel like I don't have any purpose in life."

Kat snorted. Tried to turn it into a sneeze.

Then decided it would be better to leave than to stay.

She headed back to her room, her prison, her refuge. And, as she walked along the white halls, the white walls, she reconsidered her new strategy. Lying. She suddenly realized that she probably wasn't the only one to give bullshit answers. But, if she kept it up, she thought, eventually she was going to believe her own shit. It was like dotting her I's with little hearts. What you did *did* change how you felt. And what you thought.

Maybe that was the point.

Mid-week, Holly sat down across from Kat in the cafeteria. Kat was surprised. Usually it was the other way around. Given the constant rumble in the room, she saw, but didn't hear, the slam of her tray onto the table.

"So who's your psychiatrist?" Holly got right to the point.

"Gagnon."

"What's he like?"

"Oh, we have lots of discussions," Kat said. "He finds me interesting. Entertaining. He gets this smile on his face that just makes me want to smack him. Reminds me of my father. Every time I opened my mouth, made a good argument, he'd look at me with this amused expression on his face. Like he was seeing a monkey on a bicycle." She took a bite of her tuna sandwich. "Yours?"

"Used to be Burch. Now it's fucking McIntosh."

"*Fucking* McIntosh?"

"Today, he says 'So I see you're quite the health nut. Says here you can do a hundred push-ups.' He was reading my file. First session."

Kat nodded.

"Then he says 'So I guess that means you could beat me at arm wrestling.'"

"What'd you say?"

"I just agreed. And he went fuckin' nuts! Told me that that was an inappropriate response for a lady."

Kat considered that. "What's inappropriate about it? You agreed. With what a man said. Isn't that— Oh wait— You were supposed to lie. To protect his fragile ego."

"Fucking men!" Holly tore a hunk from her bread roll. "They *are* so fucking fragile, aren't they! They need encouragement to goddamn *do* anything, then they need constant cheerleading while they do it, and then they need unending praise and congratulations when they've done it."

Kat grinned. Darryl, no doubt.

"So then what did you say?"

"'Oh, sorry, I mean, no sir, I surely couldn't beat you at arm wrestling, I who have spent several hours a day working out to create this strong, flexible, and fit body could *never* beat a desk jockey slash couch potato like you. Never happen. Sir.'"

"Was that wise?"

"Hell, no. So if I start wearing pink frills and gushing about flower arrangements, you'll know he's put me on estrogen injections."

Kat grinned, then realized she was serious.

"He would do that? He *could* do that? Give you estrogen injections? Against your wishes?"

Besides which, an increase in estrogen wouldn't make Holly wear pink frills and gush about flower arrangements. Would it?

Holly nodded. "If it's considered medically necessary, in the best interests of my health, they feel not only *allowed* to do it, but *obligated* to do it."

"Wow."

"Yeah."

"Funny, they never thought that about abortion."

Despite the recent breakthrough conversation, Kat continued to get a cold shoulder from Holly. So she hung around with Dell and occasionally Liz. But they too were … wary. So when she wasn't attending a class or a group session—she vowed to be a quiet little mouse in both; she figured it was better than outright lying and, honestly, since there was no way she could turn into June Cleaver overnight (or ever), it was the best she could do—she spent most of her time in her room. And, of course, outside, during the increasingly precious hour in the morning and again in the afternoon—walking, walking …

"Just before I was arrested," Liz said, the four of them were having lunch together, which was the only time they weren't guarded around Kat, "a Big Burgers manager told someone I know who works there, a lesbian, that she needed to dress in more gender-appropriate clothing in order to receive a promotion."

"I'm not surprised," Holly said. "I used to work in an office. In Ottawa. It's not official, but you're frowned upon if you don't perform femininity."

"Well, it *couldn't've* been official," Kat said. "Especially in a *government* office."

"Until now," Dell said.

Yeah.

"Remember when airline attendants had to wear make-up?" Kat said. "If they were female?"

"And if they were male, they *couldn't* wear make-up," Dell added.

"We're right back there, aren't we," she sighed.

Yeah.

"Men couldn't, can't, wear jewelry either," Dell said. "At least, not ear-rings. Finger rings are okay."

"It's all so arbitrary, isn't it."

"Until 1993, women couldn't wear pants in the Senate," Liz said. "Until 2013, in Paris, it was illegal for women to wear pants anywhere. And today, in Khartoum, wearing pants can get you whipped."

"Upskirting must be big in Khartoum," Holly commented.

Kat looked at her, blankly.

"Upskirting is what they call it when men surreptitiously hold their phones— You know phones have cameras nowadays, right?"

"She does now," Dell grinned.

"Well, they hold their phones below a woman's skirt to get a picture of their crotch."

Kat was stunned.

"Why? I mean that can't possibly be sexually titillating. Can it? Ugly panty hose over thick thigh ..."

"They post them online."

Kat considered that. "Again, why?"

"It's intended to be an invasion of privacy," Liz explained. "A humiliation."

Kat considered that. "Fucking men," she concluded.

Then added, a moment later, "They really should make up their minds. First we show too much, then we don't show enough."

"I'm not sure that's the point," Holly said.

So what was the point? Simply that men and women must dress differently?

"In Somalia, it's illegal to wear a bra," Liz said. "And here, it's illegal not to."

"What?" That was Kat. Of course.

Holly turned to her. "Remember that woman with a bilateral mastectomy who was told she had to wear a bathing suit top. At a public swimming pool?"

"Yeah ..."

"Well … now it's illegal for women not to wear a bra. Anywhere."

Kat hadn't known that. She tried to work out the logic. Ah. Women are sexual. Therefore burka *and* therefore bikini.

"In Iraq, they stone women to death if they're not wearing gloves," Liz continued.

"Yeah, but Iraq—"

But what.

It finally occurred to Kat that there had to be an underground, some sort of rebel core. Given the rampant bullshitting that she thought must surely be going on. She thought about how to ask Liz, and maybe Dell, without putting them at risk. She started looking hard in each class she attended, for Morse code in the clicking of the knitting needles, for coded messages in the small talk during the quilting. But if there was any such thing, Kat didn't see it.

"So, did you see the third season of *The Handmaid's Tale?*" Kat casually asked the woman beside her at the next sewing class. Several of them were standing around a large table, laying pattern pieces onto several yards of fabric.

"I wouldn't be caught *dead* watching such filth," the woman replied, staring intently at Kat.

"Actually, I heard that Atwood *was* dead," one of the other women said. "Assassinated."

"No, she's just in hiding."

"And … good riddance to her."

Kat finally figured it out. Maybe. Sort of. But didn't know what to do about it. No one approached her in the cafeteria or while she was out walking.

Maybe she was simply, intentionally, being excluded. And she couldn't blame them, whoever 'them' were. A lifetime of being upfront and direct meant she wasn't any good at deception. Apart from her pathetic performance in the Childless group, she certainly hadn't demonstrated any acting ability. If included, she'd put the whole group, whatever their plan, at risk.

And that's when it hit her. Quiet little mouse wouldn't be good enough. But no matter how perfect her performance, they'd never believe her. 'They' being the staff. The people in control of her future. Her attitude, her demeanour, needed a complete make-over. And she wasn't sure she could do that. Not now, not at sixty. Not convincingly.

She wasn't ever getting out of here. Not through the front door.

She called her lawyer the next day.

"Any news on the community treatment thing you mentioned?"

"Sorry, no. I'm still waiting for your psychiatrist to get back to me. As I explained, he has to agree that you meet the criteria."

She decided to mention it at their next session. Perhaps she could persuade him that it would be an interesting experiment. An amusing experiment, even.

YoungUn: So when were those Gender Recognition Acts finally repealed? Is that the right word?

RiseUp: Just a few years ago. You're a high school student, aren't you? So you would have been in grade school. Hopefully, that explains your ... ignorance.

    ↳ **Academe:** Though a thorough and accurate history of this stuff isn't likely to be in any of her university courses either.

GenJen: YoungUn, after many petitions and demonstrations, that probably didn't have any real influence, the powers that be finally decided that it was fraudulent for men to say they were women and so gain access to women's shelters, prisons, sports, and so on. The Gender Fraud laws replaced the Gender Recognition Acts.

    ↳ **RiseUp:** Google the "Gender Hurts!" protest.

        ↳ **Shazaam:** I was there! "Gender Hurts!" "Gender is a Violation of Human Rights!"

        ↳ **SeeJaneScream:** Me too! "Fuck Femininity!"

RadFemRocks: And unfortunately carried over the same misunderstanding of sex and gender.

DrWho: Or they do understand the difference, but believe the two are, or should be, aligned. There is nothing fraudulent about women being 'masculine' and men being 'feminine' unless you subscribe to that alignment.

Carol33: I for one applaud the repeal of the Gender Recognition Acts. It's insane for a man to insist that he's a woman and that if the staff doesn't wax his testicles, it's a human rights abuse.

Abby8: I agree, but they've gone too far the other way.

Word: No, it's not that they've gone too far, it's that they're still, again, confusing sex and gender. It should have been called the Sex Recognition Act. And the thing is you can't say you're female when you're male. Well, you can, but you'd be lying. Or misinformed about biology. Which is why they should have created a Sex Fraud crime. Not a Gender Fraud crime. Because now they're including people who— Well, there's the problem. It's impossible to *commit* gender fraud, because there's no gender 'reality' in the first place. It's not like one is born masculine and then acts fraudulently by behaving feminine.

    ↳ **SeeJaneScream:** Well put, Word!

Dick: But we got rid of all the transwomen! Isn't that what you ladies wanted? The TERFs among you?

RadFemRocks: Got rid of? How? You've just made it illegal to separate gender from sex. And in the process, you've intensified binary gender. Because the more one moves from the extremes, the closer one moves to the middle, the more one risks being accused of crossing over, the more one risks being arrested.

> ↳ **SeeJaneScream:** And well put, RadFemRocks! It's now *illegal* to separate gender from sex!

Dick: Well, making something illegal does tend to decrease its occurrence, wouldn't you agree?

> ↳ **Academe:** Not always. Didn't prohibiting the use of alcohol just force it underground?

> ↳ **SeeJaneScream:** And are you sure that making it illegal was the best solution? Mightn't it have been better to just make it immoral? Socially unacceptable?

BigRed: Besides which, we weren't against anyone being *transgender*! We were against men who adopted feminine behaviours and appearances *calling themselves women*. And insisting on access to women-only spaces. They acted like they were entitled to do whatever they want, to go wherever they want. They acted like men. They didn't have female reproductive physiology. They didn't have XX chromosomes.

GenJen: And of course some of us were particularly angry because they adopted the most silly and stereotypical behaviours and appearances.

RadFemRocks: Explain to me, Dick, why we *need* gender. Because the best solution would have been to get rid of gender altogether! Then people wouldn't feel compelled to become transexual in order to be transgender. In fact, *then* 'trans' would lose meaning altogether! So explain. Why do we *need* gender?

Dick: It's not that we *need* gender; gender is natural. Women are naturally more passive than men, men naturally more aggressive.

    ↳ **LovesSarcasm:** Oh for dick's sake!

DrWho: Maybe, but passivity and aggression are distributed across the sexes on a continuum. Why censor the individual women who are more aggressive than the norm? And the men who are more passive than the norm?

RiseUp: And surely what is natural is to some extent malleable. Surely how passive and how aggressive one is is determined not *solely* by, what, one's sexual hormones? That's what you're saying, right? Surely passivity and aggression are to some extent influenced by nurture, by all the social influences one is exposed to. So why insist that those attributes be aligned *solely* with sex? Aren't you then *denying* social influence? Or are you insisting people be completely *immune* so social influence? I'd suggest that both positions are untenable.

ExAcademe: And, let's back up to your fundamental position, the bedrock of your position: whatever is natural is right and good. How do you figure that? If you value consistency at all, then you also have to endorse physical violence, for surely that's natural in some cases. Surely you don't think physical violence is morally right. And unlimited reproduction—don't males *by nature* want to impregnate as many women as possible? Surely you don't think that would be morally good. Can you support an unlimited number of children? Or are you thinking it's morally acceptable for you to abandon your progeny? Make 'em then leave 'em?

RadFemRocks: And, let's turn to the elephant in the room (again): what about all the gender traits that *don't* have any basis in biology? Why should women wear dresses and skirts? Until the nineteenth century, it was convention for *men* to wear dresses and skirts. Even stockings. Though they may have called them robes and tunics. And leggings. In many countries, men still wear robes. Saudi Arabia, Kuwait, Yemen. Long hair for men was very acceptable here in the 1960s. And why not? Explain to me how the length of one's head hair, and make-up, and favorite colors, and career choice—is inextricably related to one's chromosomes.

Dick: You're overthinking it. It's just a way of easily distinguishing between men and women.

    ↳ **SeeJaneScream:** No, you're *under*thinking it!

RadFemRocks: And why do we need to do that? Distinguish between men and women?

Dick: Isn't it obvious?

RadFemRocks: No. Except in a medical context, why do we need to distinguish between men and women?

    ↳ **LovesSarcasm:** Because otherwise dick wouldn't know who to fuck.

I'm wondering," Kat began, at her next session with Dr. Gagnon, "I mean, I understand it's possible to get a community treatment order, and—"

"Well, Katherine," he interrupted her, "if you can't even follow the rules of this facility, I don't see how you can be trusted to follow the rules of a community treatment order."

Fair enough.

"But," she had to try, "I'm not sick. I'm not confused. Gender is a *social construct*. At its base, it's *arbitrary*. And now, it's rigidly aligned with sex and used to subordinate women. It's *harmful*. Don't you see that? Being feminine, doing feminine, cripples us. Physically. *Psychologically*. What rational, thoughtful person would endorse it? Accept it? *Embrace* it?" What *psychologist* would accept it? *Embrace* it?

Days passed. Weeks. Perhaps months. Kat didn't really know. She started having panic attacks, difficulty thinking, difficulty remembering. She lost another ten pounds. It's the stress, she thought. Her body must be flooded with cortisol, interfering with her capacity to function. If her system hadn't already been compromised by the loss of Tassi, perhaps she could have handled— No, living in such close quarters with so many people, not having access to the forest, the water, knowing she might never again— Not to mention wearing dresses and skirts every day, putting on make-up every day, pretending to be someone she most definitely wasn't, someone she most definitely didn't want to be …

RiseUp: Did anyone see the news about Timmins? Apparently, they've made hundreds of arrests for violations of the new Gender Fraud legislation. For those of you who don't know, Timmins is pretty far north. Population under 50,000. So they're not just doing this in the big cities anymore.

LovesScience: Yes, they've reached Yellowknife too.

BigRed: And it's not just trans they're arresting; lesbians are targetted too.

SeeJaneScream: My aunt was arrested yesterday, and she's neither. She just doesn't do the whole femme thing.

LovesScience: Where are they putting all these women? The mental health facilities are surely full by now, and the prisons were bursting even *before* all this.

DrWho: They've been building new facilities. But I agree, there can't be enough room!

Abby8: Maybe they're appropriating other spaces.

↳ LovesScience: Oh my god. They've been closing down university departments. They must be making room in the dorms. Oh god, how could we not see it?

BigRed: I hear they're giving them electroshock therapy.

GenJen: Oh no. We have to do something.

RiseUp: But what? I mean, what more? We're blogging like crazy to raise awareness—those of us whose blogs haven't been shut down. We've started a petition to repeal the law. We've lobbied our representatives. We've held protests. What more can we do?

ExAcademe: Wait for it to happen and then sue.

RiseUp: That would be too late.

ExAcademe: Agreed. But.

↳ BigRed: Funny how no one ever said Bruce Jenner needed electroshock therapy when he became Caitlyn. And no one ever would. But when *women* became transgender—hell, women—some women, the *best* women—were, I reiterate, *always* transgender—then yes, let's bring out the electrodes.

↳ Abby8: But men who became trans are being arrested. Now.

↳ BigRed: And as many men who are just not performing masculinity as women not performing femininity?

↳ **Abby8:** Well, maybe there's just not as many of them.

↳ **ThinkAboutIt:** And that's interesting. Ask yourself why.

GenJen: It's for your own good, they'll tell us.

Carol33: I don't believe it. I mean, they wouldn't. Electroshock??

SeeJaneScream: Sure they would. Back in 1972, Chesler said that mental institutions were used to punish women who rebelled against the constraints of femininity. *The Yellow Wallpaper.* For one.

One day, Kat saw Dell sitting alone on one of the benches in the yard, so she approached her.

"So I've been thinking—"

Dell burst out laughing. "When are you not?"

She grinned. "Yeah."

"But you know, that's good. I never told you before, but I've always admired your capacity for thought. More people should be like you. Thinking about things all the time. What a wonderful world that would be, yeah? My mother always said that. Sang it, actually. 'What a wonderful world …'" Dell sang. Horribly. "I should have listened to her. Because it is. A wonderful world." She turned to Kat and smiled.

Kat stared at her. Aghast. Then managed to say, simply, "Well, aren't you a long-winded Little Miss Sunshine today!"

Dell stopped smiling, then burst out sobbing.

Kat knew immediately. They'd increased her estrogen dosage.

"I don't know *who* I am anymore!" Dell confessed. "I don't know *what* I am! Other than a freak! A total fuck-up!"

"No, you're not," Kat said. "I've always admired you too …"

But there was no consoling her.

"Have either of you seen Liz lately?" Kat asked next day at lunch. It had occurred to her that she hadn't seen her in a while. Though how long 'a while' was, she wasn't sure.

Dell shook her head. Tearless. For now. "Maybe she was released."

Holly looked up sharply. "Do you know when she was admitted?"

"No," Kat replied.

"Maybe she killed herself," Holly said then, more to her lasagna than to Kat or Dell.

"She didn't seem depressed last time we spoke." But even as she said it, Kat realized that many suicides surprise the people closest to them. And Kat wasn't particularly close to Liz.

How many shoelaces would it take to make a successful noose? No, they didn't have shoelaces. Even her nurse's shoes and Dell's walking shoes had velcro fasteners. Had she smuggled something from the kitchen? The sewing classroom?

More likely, she thought, she'd escaped. Her lesbian network had come to the rescue and—and she didn't tell anyone. Didn't tell Kat.

She understood. It would have been a risk. Telling other people. Telling Kat.

And as she'd just noted, they weren't particularly close.

"Or worse." Dell shoved her plate away from her. Most of it uneaten.

Kat looked at her and was about to ask what could be worse than killing yourself, but then remembered one of their previous lunch conversations.

"You think the staff … killed her? Caused her death?"

Dell shrugged.

Kat also pushed her plate away. Because if they were … arranging patient deaths …

Surely she was in line.

The day after that, shortly before lunch, Holly's counsellor escorted her back to their room. That in itself was alarming. But—

"Holly?" No response.

"Is she okay?" Kat demanded of the counsellor. "What did you do to her?"

"She'll be fine. It's for her own good."

Kat wanted to smack her. Fortunately, the woman left as soon as Holly was in the room and sitting on her bed.

"Holly? Are you okay? What happened?"

Holly just sat on her bed. Her face a blank. A blank slate.

She knew immediately that Holly had had electroshock therapy. And she lost it. Started screaming at the camera and throwing her cleansers, exfoliators, and moisturizers, her mascara, eye shadow, and eyeliner, her lipsticks, her hairbrush— She picked up her chair—

She had to escape. She realized this now. Or again.

"Stupid, stupid, stupid," she started pacing, berating herself. She'd just made threats. They had them on tape. Not that that would matter much, given everything else they had on record about her. She tried to think …

And then, a few days later, when she was outside, walking about, luxuriating in the strong wind, remembering trees swaying in the forest, distant cracks as the brittle ones fell—the power went off. While the automated gate was closing. She made a run for it.

Time was she could do the 100 in thirteen seconds. She figured the distance to the gate was less than that, because otherwise there was no way she'd've been able to *see* that the gate had stopped. At half-open. Even so, she hoped she had twice that time before the back-up generator powered on.

She heard Dell start wailing. She stumbled, looked back, saw her in hysterics, then—smiled. Even in estrogen overdrive, Dell wouldn't've been afraid of the wind. It was a diversion.

I'll come back for you, I'll get you, and Holly, and whoever else, I'll get you out, somehow, Kat promised as she kept sprinting. Well, running. She was almost there. Almost— DAMN! She heard the roar of the generator, she saw the gate resume closing, she—made it! Got thumped on the way through when the long dress got snagged and pulled her back before it ripped nearly in two, but she was through! YES!

She kept running. Get out of sight, she told herself, don't slow down yet, you can do this. She saw a curve in the road, in the distance. Get around that curve, you can do this—

She didn't know the infirmary nurse had injected a tracking chip.